Black Orchid

Robert V. Wadden, Jr.

ISBN: 978-1-62420-550-7

Credits
Cover Artist: Designs by Ms G
Editor: Sherry Derr-Wille

Printed in the United States of America

One
Mu Jin Lounge, LA Chinatown

The place was what I had hoped, loaded with kitschy Asian atmosphere. There was a rosewood bar with a carved dragon and a green onyx countertop. Small golden dragon sculptures flanked a glass and rosewood cabinet behind the bar used to house the liquor. Red silk hangings on the walls with black Chinese characters and brass casts of Buddha in every alcove all added to the atmosphere. The floor was black-painted hardwood, the cocktail tables were rosewood with carved dragons, birds around the edges, and legs carved like lion's paws. The matching rosewood chairs were upholstered in red fabric to match the wall hangings. It looked like a set from an old Fu Manchu movie, very cool.

The Mu Jin lounge was on an obscure block of Alpine Street on the second story above a Vietnamese/Chinese restaurant. Except for the small sign by the door leading to the stairway you would never have known it was there.

I heard about it from a girl at the office who shares my taste for the obscure and kitschy, and as always, she was right on target with this place. It was an easy Dash ride from the building on Figueroa where I rented an office from a big law firm. It seemed perfect for an after-work drink. With any luck I would have a drink then grab a quick bite at some Chinatown eatery before heading back to Hermosa in the wake of rush hour traffic.

I grabbed a table. I hate sitting at the bar in places; too often people expect you to chat with them and I wasn't in the mood. In fact, I am never in the mood. The only other people in the bar were a middle-aged Asian couple at another table and a woman sitting at the bar.

From the back the woman looked pretty hot: long black hair, nice figure, but I couldn't see her face. Not that it mattered. I'd never picked up a woman in a bar, or anywhere else in the thirty-six years of my life. I was pretty sure I never would.

I figured in a place like this a mai tai would be the right choice, a drink as kitschy as my surroundings. I ordered from a gray-haired Chinese waiter in a white jacket. While I waited, I checked my phone, saw I already had four e-mails from clients even though it was almost six. They should be heading home to their families.

As the waiter arrived with the drink, the girl at the bar turned around and glanced at me. She was way beyond hot. She wore a blue sleeveless silk dress to match her huge sapphire blue eyes. Her cheekbones were defined and her skin was pale in contrast to her long, silky, jet black hair. I immediately wrote her off as way out of my league: probably more like out of my universe.

The drink was good, the background flavor of the white and dark rums was pleasantly discernable behind the sweetness of the fruit juice and the almond flavor of the orgeat syrup. A mai tai may be a corny drink, but when made right it can also be pretty tasty and easily intoxicating.

As I reflected on the virtues of the mai tai I noticed, to my terror, the dark-haired woman at the bar had gotten up and seemed to be heading my way. I hoped she was on her way to the exit, maybe the ladies' room, taking an indirect route. Instead she walked right up to my table. I immediately saw I had underestimated her beauty.

Her skirt was above her knees, revealing a pair of long, lovely, shapely legs. Her eyes were bigger and more astonishing seeing her up close. She was tall, maybe five foot six or five foot seven, and could not have been much older than twenty-six or twenty-seven. She was curvy in a lanky sort of way, if that makes any sense, long legged but with soft round hips and distinctive breasts. She wore little jewelry, just a plain silver chain around her neck from which hung what I assumed was a genuine sapphire. There was no ring of any kind on her left hand. The blue of her silk dress matched the dazzling blue of her eyes and drew attention to them.

"Hi, I'm Ariella," she said without a trace of self-consciousness.

"Fred, Fred Cornwall."

"Can I buy you a drink, Fred?"

"Of course, please sit down," I said, trying not to sound terrified, which I was.

She smoothed her dress and sat down opposite me.

"I love this place. It feels like a movie set. I come here whenever I'm downtown," she said with an easy smile.

"Funny, that's just what I was thinking, like the set of an old Fu Manchu movie, almost like a self-parody of what it's supposed to be. I've never been here before. Somebody at the office told me about it and it definitely lived up to her billing."

So far, I thought, I was doing okay keeping up my side of the conversation. I'm not ugly or fat or anything, just very ordinary looking, five foot ten, one hundred and seventy-five pounds, dark hair, clear complexion, brown eyes. I guess I look my age. Somehow, I have never done well with women, only had a few girlfriends, and every single one of them dumped me.

"Where do you work, Fred?

"Over on Figueroa, I rent an office from Tester and Moyers, the big law firm."

"So, you're a lawyer? What kind of law do you practice?" Now it sounded like she was just making polite conversation.

"Business law. I have a few small business clients, a packing house, some accountants and doctors, a couple of small restaurant chains. To be honest, it's pretty boring stuff. What do you do?"

"I guess you could call me a consultant of sorts. I also have a lot of investments. That's why I was downtown today seeing my lawyer about offshoring as much of my money as I can."

"Wow, you must be doing pretty well if you're concerned about shifting money offshore?"

"I'm doing very well, but to be honest it's more about privacy. My line of work demands a certain level of discretion."

"What exactly is it you consult on?"

She smiled as if the question amused her a lot. "It's complicated. I guess you could say it's a kind of human resources, risk management sort of thing. It's hard to explain. If I ever get to know you better maybe I could explain it more." The smile lingered as she paused. "So, Fred, where do you live?"

"Hermosa Beach. In a way that's why I'm here, just killing time waiting for the traffic to ebb, it's a miserable drive."

Just then the old waiter in the white jacket arrived with another mai tai for me and a white wine for the girl. I gulped down the last of my first one so he could clear the glass. The sudden rush of rum to my brain loosened my tongue and fortified my courage. "If you're free, maybe we could grab a bite to eat at some place here in Chinatown?"

"Sadly, Fred, I have to be someplace in just a little over an hour but it sounds like an idea. Why don't you give me your card and I can give you a call when I'm free? I have to go out of the country for a while on a consulting job. I do a lot of my work overseas. When I get back, I may have some time. I'll let you know. By the way, what kind of music do you like?"

This seemed like a trick question to me. One I wanted to answer correctly to give her the answer she wanted. I was just drunk enough to realize I had no idea what that might be, so I just told the truth.

"Jazz," I said, "real hard core be-bop, Charlie Parker, Lester Young, Clifford Brown. I like all kinds of music, too," I added lamely.

"I had you pegged as a jazz fan. Just a wild guess, an instinct. I tend to trust my instincts. We definitely share a taste in music, Fred. I like that."

Her smile was so dazzling it made my stomach queasy. I wondered if I had given the correct answer or she was just being polite. A friend once told me the best way to deal with women was just to be honest with them. I never bought that, but maybe he was right after all. Even so, she brushed off my dinner invitation, clearly was not about to give me her number or even her last name, so I was prepared to take the well-worn path to the dugout after striking out.

"I'd love to stay and talk for a while, but I have to get to Beverly Hills. It will take forever to get there. Let me have one of your cards and

I'll get in touch when I have a chance."

I pulled out my card case and gave her one with a sinking heart.

"Well, thanks for the drink, maybe we'll be talking soon?"

"Maybe we will," she said with another dazzling smile.

She stood up, turned and walked toward the stairs. I could hear the swishing of her silk skirt as she moved, swaying her hips gently. A faint whiff of Chanel remained in the air. From the back she was as graceful as a cheetah despite her spiked heels.

This was a woman who was comfortable in her own skin. I had no idea why she bothered with me. Maybe she was just playing with me out of boredom or to show she could play me. I doubted I would ever see or hear from her again.

Two
FBI Regional Headquarters, Miramar, Fla

Gabriel Osorio was the deputy finance minister for the country of Venezuela, or had been up until a few hours ago. He expired in a limousine on the way to the Dade County airport. Cause of death was ventricular arrhythmia depleting oxygen from his system resulting in cardiac arrest. Osorio had no history of heart problems. He was fifty-two years old and ostensibly in excellent health. He was also about to defect from the Venezuelan government and was on his way to Washington, D.C. to meet with Treasury Department officials. It was suspected Osorio had information about government funds which the leaders of the Venezuelan government had diverted into personal accounts and investments. He was not planning on traveling back to Venezuela.

It was possible the sudden heart failure was caused by a previously undetected health problem but FBI Special Agent Chandler Diaz doubted that. He was waiting for the toxicology report which he expected would show some sort of poison in Osorio's blood stream and possibly some information about how that poison had been administered.

Osorio had both his personal security and two FBI agents with him. The opportunity to poison him would have been limited. If Osorio had indeed been poisoned, and Diaz's instincts told him he had been, the killer must have been highly skilled.

Osorio's security guards were in custody and being interrogated by Diaz's team. They had been with Osorio for years; there was nothing to lead him to think either one of them would have been responsible.

As he headed down to interrogation, he was handed a copy of the expedited toxicology report. Significant traces of aconite had been found in Osorio's system. An addendum to the report indicated a small puncture mark had been found on Osorio's back. It was the right size for an injection point. Diaz knew a dose of twenty to forty milligrams of aconite, also known as "wolfsbane," would have been enough to induce ventricular arrhythmia rather quickly and result in death within a half hour or less.

Now that he knew the means of assassination, Diaz would get the toxicology people to give him an estimate of the dose which would give him a fairly precise timeframe. He and his team could go back, retrace Osorio's movements during that time period, interview witnesses and view any security camera footage that might indicate with whom Osorio had contact during those crucial minutes.

With any luck they might focus on a perpetrator. If they could find the perpetrator, they might be able to find out who was behind the murder and why. Of course, Diaz had a pretty good idea who would have wanted Osorio dead. It was the handful of Venezuelan government officials whose ransacked millions were in danger of being seized by the U.S. government if Osorio could identify their location and provenance. The loss of those funds and the political fallout that would ensue when an unfriendly U.S. government notified the people of Venezuela their tax money was being diverted by corrupt officials was a strong motive to kill the man with the information.

Diaz knew there would be no way to trace the provenance of the aconite since it could be derived from a number of common flowering plants. There would be no pharmaceutical origin which could be used to trace a buyer. The poison was likely made in someone's kitchen.

Diaz worked out of FBI headquarters in Washington D.C., in charge of a task force assigned to high profile homicides and organized crime. Osorio's death fit that profile and the local police were more than happy to turn the case over to him. He was now forty-two and had worked for the FBI since finishing law school at twenty-five. He was smart, diligent, avoided Agency politics and loved his job. He had never married or had children, ending every serious relationship. His fervent belief was his job came first, always would. He would make a poor husband and father as a result. He did get lonely on occasion. He usually worked long, intense hours, rarely having time to reflect on his life choices. If you asked him, he would have told you he was happy.

As he headed down the hall to interrogation, he whistled *Cucala*, his favorite Celia Cruz tune his Cuban father had played over and over when he was a boy. Diaz knew enough to have a plan and, in his career, a diligent plan carefully executed was successful more often than not. Criminals were usually not that smart: at least, not as smart as he was.

Three
Hermosa Beach

Lindsay looked forward to the Sunday morning beach volleyball games at the Third Street nets. She loved the camaraderie, the good-looking guys and girls in great shape who played. She enjoyed the drinks and wings at Patrick Molloy's on Pier Plaza afterward with everybody sweaty, laughing, tired, pitchers of beer sloshing on the table, Bloody Marys, platters of spicy wings, sports on the televisions mounted on the walls. She also had to admit it was the one time in the week when she knew she would see Fred Cornwall. Occasionally he might come into Hennessey's where she waitressed. She would make sure she handled his table even if it wasn't supposed to be hers but that did not happen often.

He rarely missed a Sunday morning game, though. He wasn't the best player there. In fact, he really wasn't all that good. He wasn't the best-looking guy there. Some girls might say he was average, you know, just okay. There was something about him she really liked. He was shy, not full of himself like most guys, and he was smart. He was a lawyer who worked downtown; he made a little money she was sure. She just felt at ease with him, liked being around him.

She tried sending the message, letting him know, without being too obvious, she was interested. He never seemed to pick up on it. She did not think it was because he wasn't interested. She was cute, she knew it and had guys hitting on her all the time. She didn't want to come across like a slut and give him the wrong idea. Fred was a keeper, not a guy for a hook-up. Like a typical guy he didn't get it, couldn't pick up on the signs, was clueless. She knew she would have to work harder to let him know she wanted to get to know him better. She needed to let him know she was a smart girl, not just a dumb waitress. She just didn't want to telegraph it.

That Sunday he was there in baggy blue trunks with a white hibiscus flower print. Whenever Lindsay served, she aimed it right at Fred. Lindsay could play: she was a natural athlete. Her serves inevitably twisted Fred around as he flailed at the ball. She didn't want to embarrass him though, just get his attention, but it did not seem to work.

Later at Patrick Molloy's, she rushed to get the seat next to him. He nursed his drink and looked around the table, never the one to initiate conversation.

"Hey, Fred," said Lindsay, "how was your week?"

"Just the usual bullshit," he answered as he sipped his Moscow Mule out of a heavy metal cup. "How about you? Did you have a good week?"

"It was kind of a grind," she answered happily. "I had four days of split shifts but I managed some beach time, got some color," she said, extending her burnished brown arms for him to admire. "I bet that's better than having to work downtown with no beach break?"

"On hot days it's definitely a drag. Some days I try to work through lunch and leave early but most days this week I was stuck in the office until late. I did discover a truly kitschy bar in Chinatown one night after work."

"No kidding." She thought this sounded lame but she didn't know what else to say, she wanted him to keep talking.

"Yeah, there were Buddhas everywhere, carved dragons, red upholstery, rosewood tables, a huge rosewood bar with a green stone top with dragons all over it."

"Sounds great. I'd love to see it."

"I can give you the address. It's kinda hard to find but worth the trip. I met this amazing woman there."

Lindsay's stomach twisted into a knot.

"The girl was really beautiful, tall, pale, dark haired and curvy with the most amazing blue eyes. The woman actually bought me a drink, was very mysterious, wouldn't tell me much about herself, seemed loaded, wearing really expensive clothes, talking about offshoring her assets."

"Did you get her number?"

"No."

Lindsay's stomach suddenly relaxed.

"I didn't even get her last name."

Lindsay smiled.

"She took my card, said she would call me but I doubt I'll ever see her again. Still, she was amazingly beautiful."

Four
Phillipe's, Downtown L.A.

Phillipe's is an old sandwich joint on the edge of Chinatown. It is very funky, sawdust on the floor, counter service, vats of their signature mustard on every table. They are famous for their French dip sandwiches. Eugene and I got a booth in the back. He had the pork dip and I got what I always get, the lamb dip. Slices of tender lamb sliced off the leg right in front of you on a crisp French roll dipped in a rich meat broth, a great sandwich.

Eugene is Haitian, at least his parents were, so I guess that makes him Haitian-American. His ancestors lived in Haiti a lot longer than most of our ancestors lived here in the U.S. His parents came over when Francois Duvalier, AKA "Papa Doc," became president and began taking revenge on the old aristocratic families who traditionally controlled Haiti.

Eugene was a slender, elegant, man with light brown skin and short, wiry black hair on a long bullet shaped head. He had large, soft brown eyes that always looked amused and he seemed to always be holding back a laugh. He was a risk manager for one of my clients, that's how I met him. We became friends because he is such an odd duck. I have always liked odd ducks.

"What has been happening, Fred?" he asked in that slightly clipped accent of his. He was born in this country. He spoke French and Creole at home which affected the way he spoke English.

I talked a little bit about a case I was working on, a business partnership that seemed destined to split up. I was trying to negotiate a buy out on behalf of one of the partners was getting nowhere and contemplating filing an action for partition if we could not reach a settlement.

"Hey, did you ever hear from that girl you met in Chinatown a few weeks ago?"

To no surprise of my own I never received a call back from that blue-eyed beauty. I knew nothing about her, not even her last name and had no way to track her down. What would be the point anyway? If she were interested, she would have called, but why would a girl like that be interested in me? I have to admit, sheepishly, I went back to Mu Jin Lounge, not once but twice in the last couple of weeks in hopes of running into her again. Of course, no luck. I even asked the bartender about her. He smiled knowingly, said he remembered her, did not know anything about her other than she would occasionally come in, maybe once every couple of months and always ordered a white wine. Had I actually run into her I am not sure I would have had the nerve to approach her, maybe after two or three mai tais. The trips were not a complete waste. I liked the place and enjoyed the drinks and the ambiance.

"I think maybe you made this girl up," said Eugene. "She doesn't sound real at all. Really Fred, I love you to death but what would a girl like you describe see in a guy like you?"

I could not disagree with Eugene, as insulting as his good-natured comment was. In the end my life was simple, quiet, lacking in drama maybe even boring, but I like it that way. Did I really need a girlfriend? I had been sexually frustrated all my life and the few relationships I had did not do much to remedy that. So maybe I was better off the way I was.

"Eugene," I said changing the subject, "when are you going to come down to Hermosa Beach?"

I was always trying to get Eugene to visit me at home, which he would never do. We always met for lunch downtown where we both worked or sometimes for dinner at a place close to downtown, like Ti George's Chicken, one of the few Haitian restaurants in the L.A. area, one of Eugene's favorites. He hated the beach, particularly hated the South Bay.

"Fred, when I go down your way, I feel like I'm in a foreign country. All those blonde surfers and surfer girls, everyone white. I don't belong, feel like I need a passport or something. No thanks, man, I'll stick to where I have a comfort level and that's not in the beach cities, man."

We bantered for a while, ate our sandwiches and, after making plans to meet for dinner soon, went back to our respective offices.

When I got back, I had two messages from clients so I went to the file cabinet to pull their files before returning the calls and pulled out my billing sheet.

The receptionist I shared with about five other lawyers renting offices from the firm buzzed through to me. "There's a woman on the phone named Ariella, she says you know her."

The lamb dip sandwich in my stomach started doing flips. "Put her through," I said.

"Hey, Fred, it's Ariella. Remember me from the Mu Jin Lounge?"

Five
Singapore

The crime scene was a bloody mess. An elevator with three bodies riddled with holes made by eight-millimeter slugs, blood everywhere, the bodies disfigured. The victims were Singapore businessman Vi Li Tsing and his two bodyguards. The killer stood on the roof of the elevator car and lifted the service trapdoor to fire down onto the passengers. The bodyguards had no chance to draw their weapons and Tsing was a sitting duck.

For Diaz there were several questions. How had the killer gotten away? Was the elevator moving when the shooting started? Where was the weapon? What motive would anyone have for killing Tsing? He was exceedingly wealthy, certainly worth several hundred million dollars. His only heirs were his wife and fourteen-year-old son who were already enjoying the benefits of Tsing's wealth. They appeared to have no other motive for killing him.

Tsing's marriage was stable and he was not known to even have a mistress, rather unusual for a Singapore businessman. No one within his company stood to benefit from his death and while he had business rivals, these rivalries were not tinged with bad blood. The Singapore police asked the FBI for assistance. Diaz had, by luck, good or bad, he was not sure, been already in the city for an international law enforcement conference.

He was still working on the Osorio killing. His plan had not uncovered any useful information. Forensics estimated about a twenty-five-milligram dose of aconite, which meant the dose would have been administered forty to forty-five minutes before the time of death.

They tracked Osorio's movements in that time window to no avail. Osorio ate breakfast in the hotel restaurant, returned to his room alone to pack and locked the door behind him.

His guards went to their rooms to pack and the FBI agents were waiting in the lobby.

Security video showed no one else entering or leaving Osorio's room while he was inside packing.

A bellhop came to the room to take his bags. Osorio went down, caught his limousine to the airport and died on the way. They carefully checked the bellhop, who had an opportunity to administer the poison in his brief encounter with the victim. He was an elderly Cuban. Diaz himself questioned him in Spanish. He had no connection to Osorio or Venezuela. The old man did not have the look or feel of a professional killer. Diaz's instincts told him the man was innocent.

Usually when Diaz had a plan it resulted in something, if not a solution to the puzzle, at least enough information to head the investigation in a direction. With Osorio he had nothing.

Now the Singapore police wanted his help on a murder even more unlikely to be solved, one that did not even have a discernible motive.

Diaz loved puzzles. As a boy, he had thrived on mystery novels by everyone from Georges Simenon, P. D. James, and Ruth Rendell, to more literary types like Raymond Chandler and Patricia Highsmith. Once he started work at the FBI, he discovered real life was nothing like the plots of those novels.

Much of the secret to success was dogged procedural work. Endlessly reviewing surveillance videos for the smallest thing out of place, interviewing witnesses who knew nothing or thought they did, reviewing financial records. Correspondence, e-mails, fingerprints. It was hard work, much of it numbingly boring. In the end every crime was still a puzzle and the better it was covered up, the more challenging a puzzle it became.

Diaz's father was a Cuban plumber. He came as a young man during the Mariel Boat Lift. He met Diaz's mother, a young African-American woman working as a maid in a Miami Marriott, not long after.

His father was a happy man, always singing, listening to music, never complaining, accepting hardships and discrimination.

Lynn, his mother, a calm, quiet woman, suffered from severe depression. When he was fourteen, she was shot and killed as a bystander during a robbery of a convenience store. Neither he nor his father ever quite recovered.

Her death spurred him to become a law enforcement officer, to work hard, to excel at it. He had been involved in solving quite a few murder cases. When the special unit was formed, he was a natural candidate to lead it.

For two years now his team had been involved in several dozen high profile killings. Some of the cases, like Osorio, were still open but he was successful in more than half. Some were drug cartel related, some mob related, there had even been several political killings. It was the good reputation his team earned that resulted in them being called to Singapore for the killing of a prominent and respected local businessman. It was an honor that Diaz, despite his love of challenging puzzles, could have done without.

Six
Lucques Restaurant, Los Angeles

Ariella insisted on meeting at Lucques. I'd never been. I knew it was expensive, not the place I would have chosen for a first date with someone I barely know. She said it was her treat. I have to admit I felt funny about that.

I don't think of myself as sexist. I meet plenty of female lawyers and some of them are really good. I've appeared in front of some female judges I really respect. In a dating relationship isn't the guy supposed to take the lead?

Yet here I was being asked out by a woman and her telling me she would pick up the tab. I guess I should have been happy to go to a really good restaurant and have someone else pay. I felt weird about it and wondered how much she could be able to respect me if she were the financially dominant one. Not that there was any chance of my refusing. I wanted to see her again and I could not believe she called me. Never in my life had I been on a date with a woman so beautiful. I was bummed about her paying, nervous as hell, but excited at the same time.

Lucques is in an ivy-covered building on Melrose. The chef/owner is supposed to be famous, some woman whose name I can't remember. We agreed to meet at the bar and, of course, I was early. I sat for about fifteen minutes slowly sipping a mojito, the price of which was about the same as dinner at a place in Hermosa.

When she finally came in the door, she drew the glance of every man in the room. Gliding easily on blue patent-leather spiked heels, she wore a tailored, sleeveless wool dress, blue to match her eyes. She approached me with a smile.

"Been waiting long?"

"Just got here," I gulped, trying to gain my composure.

"Well, let's get our table and go eat."

We were guided to a table in the room adjacent to the bar. There were brick walls, wood beams on the ceiling and a rustic looking fireplace at the far end of the room. It was only seven but the tables were mostly occupied and the room was not quiet.

"What are you drinking?" she asked, and ordered two more when she found out. "How has your week been?" she asked as we viewed the menu.

"I'm busy but bored, if you know what I mean."

"No, I rarely get bored. I just got back from a trip to Asia. Very successful. I made two hundred thousand dollars on the deal. I'm sorry, I don't mean to brag."

"No, that's incredible, you should feel wonderful about a deal like that."

"Thank you," she said, smiling. "Let's celebrate."

She called the wine waiter over and ordered a bottle of *Veuve Cliquot, La Grande Dame* while we finished off our mojitos.

"There's no point in making money if you can't enjoy spending it."

We spent the next few minutes pouring over the menu until we ordered. She ordered a plum salad with walnut vinaigrette, tamarind, crème fraîche garnish, sherry-braised pork belly, and a strawberry tart for dessert.

I had pan-fried soft-shell crab, grilled Sonoma lamb and a stone fruit galette.

She ordered a 2015 Chambertin that was listed on the wine list at over six hundred dollars.

I was beginning to hope she meant it when she said dinner was on her because it was shaping up to be more than my monthly office rent.

The champagne arrived and was poured. It was amazing: dry, flinty with a curious, very pleasant muskiness and plenty of body.

My friend Eugene once said that good champagne should taste

like "after-sex." Now I finally knew what he meant. I am no wine expert but this was something special and I told her so.

"I have very expensive taste." She laughed. "It's a good thing I can indulge myself. There isn't much I enjoy more than a good champagne. I grew up in a pretty modest household. My parents were Russian immigrants. My father died in an automobile accident not long before I was born and my mother never remarried, she struggled to support us, me, my brother and my grandfather, who never did learn to speak English."

"Where did you grow up?"

"Mostly Lawndale. My mother bought a condo there with the settlement money from my father's accident."

"Where are they now?"

"All dead. My brother was my twin. He was autistic, more burden for my mother and me. He died young, he couldn't cope very well and he was lost once my mother went. My mother worked very hard to provide for us but she was incredibly strict. She practically had me in a chastity belt until I was twenty and she controlled my every movement like I was under house arrest. Those were hard times. I could not be an ordinary teenager and I had a hard time at first when I finally moved out."

"Did you go away to college?"

"Not at first, I went to the local junior college for two years because we couldn't afford tuition for a four year. I finally got into UCLA, got a scholarship and moved in with some other girls in an apartment off Wilshire close to campus. I guess I was out of control for a year or two. I got it out of my system and settled down. What about you? Where did you grow up?"

"Mostly Downey. My father was a CPA, my mom worked in a fabric shop. I was an only child. I guess I had a pretty boring childhood. Went to Long Beach State, then Southwestern law school. My parents were older when they had me, my dad was forty-one, my mom thirty-six. They both passed. They are all the family I ever had. My uncles and aunts lived somewhere in the Midwest."

"You never married?"

"There's never been anybody. A few girlfriends but nobody

serious. I worked pretty hard to get myself through law school, build a practice. I haven't had a lot of time for relationships."

"I can relate to that. My work takes me all over, the U.S. and other countries. It is pretty all consuming. I think I tend to wear out the men in my life. Just a warning in case this develops into something. I guess I'm pretty demanding."

"Well, you can afford to be. You are so beautiful, I imagine most men would do anything for you," I said, blushing.

We were more than half way through the bottle of *Veuve Clicquot*. The waiter brought the first courses. I was wondering how I was ever going to drive home, knowing there was another bottle to come.

"Thank you, Fred, it's nice of you to say that. I wonder if part of my problem is that when a man is willing to do anything for me, he ends up hating himself for it in the end. Does that make any sense?"

It didn't. The alcohol had gone to my head. Two mojitos and a half bottle of champagne was not enough to get me falling down drunk, but it had definitely impaired my faculties.

She must have taken my silence for a "no" as she continued. "I mean that the few men I've been involved with in my life have tended to compromise themselves to show me how much they care. That doesn't always lead to happy endings."

Now I was totally confused. I could see compromising myself for this woman. We turned our attention to the appetizers. My soft-shell crab was excellent. Whether or not her plum salad was good, it was beautiful to look at.

By the time we finished our appetizers the conversation seemed to have lost its momentum. The champagne bottle was empty and the Chambertin had not arrived yet.

"So, you travel a lot?" I asked lamely trying to get the conversation started again.

"I do. I travel for work and I have a house in Panama I often go to after a business trip to unwind."

"Panama?"

"Yes, it's in the hills a couple of hours from Panama City. It's lovely, on a hill in the middle of a forest. I think it used to belong to some drug lord but it is very relaxing. Often there are monkeys in the trees by the pool. There are macaws, parrots and toucans. It's the perfect place to unwind after the stress of a business trip, a total escape."

"What exactly do you do on these trips?"

"Make money." She laughed. "I told you my business is very confidential. I have to respect the privacy of my clients. You're a lawyer. Can you sit here and tell me the deep, dark secrets of your clients?"

It was my turn to laugh. "My clients don't have deep, dark secrets. I'm not a criminal lawyer and all my clients are legitimate businessmen. They do deals, they buy and sell real estate, businesses, borrow money, nothing I couldn't talk about. Are your clients doing something illegal?"

"If they were, I couldn't tell you." She seemed to find this conversation amusing.

We were interrupted by the sommelier bringing the six-hundred-dollar Burgundy. She uncorked it with great formality and partially filled my glass to sniff and taste. I immediately handed it to Ariella, who, after all, had ordered it and hopefully was paying for it. Her smile told me I scored points with her by the gesture.

She swirled the wine slowly, sniffed it carefully and took a tiny sip. She nodded to the sommelier who took Ariella's glass and put it in front of me before pouring, then filled the glass I gave to her. The wine was a revelation. It tasted of raspberries and cherries, intensely flavored, full of fruit, not sweet at all.

"If I continue to hang out with you, I may turn into a wine snob. These are some wonderful wines you've picked tonight."

She smiled, obviously pleased at the compliment, which was entirely genuine.

The entrees arrived and we began to eat. The food was, unsurprisingly, delicious. The lamb was cooked rare, it was moist and tender. She gave me a bite of her sherry-braised pork belly which was amazing, sweet and rich at the same time.

"My first real love affair was with a teacher at UCLA," she said, starting back up on the theme we had begun before the wine and food came. "He must have been at least twenty-five years older than me, still very handsome, distinguished looking, very bright and cultured. I learned a lot from him. In a lot of ways, he was like the father I never got to have, a mentor but a lover as well." She trained her huge blue eyes on me to gauge my reaction.

"So, whatever happened to him?"

"He died."

"While you two were in a relationship?"

"As a matter of fact, yes. It was very sad."

"Wow, he died young then. What happened?"

"Someone shot him. For a while the police thought it might be his wife but they never arrested anyone."

"He was married?"

"Seventeen years. It was never really a problem for us though. We were discreet and I don't think either of us really wanted it to get serious. His wife never found out about us. He didn't plan to leave his wife and I didn't want him to. It was just for fun but sad it had to end that way."

"Why would anyone want to shoot him?"

"Maybe somebody wasn't happy with their grade in his Russian literature class," she said with a crooked smile.

"Did the police know about you and him?"

"No, I told you we were very discreet. He had done this before with other students. He knew how to behave to avoid trouble with his wife and the administration. He taught me a lot."

"Is that why you won't give me your phone number, tell me where you live, or even tell me your last name?" I blurted out realizing that my tongue had been loosened by all the excellent wine and it was coming out all wrong.

She just seemed to be amused.

"I am very careful about my phone number. I'm sorry, but I have good reasons which I can't explain right now. I actually live in San Pedro, not too far away from you. As for a last name, I use a number of different ones. You could have your pick, but for now, let's call me Ariella Smith. Does that make you happy, Fred?" Her smile, as she said this, was sarcastic.

"You use different last names? Really, are you involved in something illegal?"

She laughed out loud at this. "Do I look like a criminal, Fred? Anyway, if I were involved in something criminal, would I tell you?"

She took a moment to drink the last of the Chambertin in her glass, I reached to pour her more but realized the bottle was already empty.

"I will confess, Fred, that I am doing some questionable things by keeping my money offshore and in shell corporation bank accounts. I bet I pay less taxes than you?"

"Is that the reason for the multiple last names?"

"Could be. Any way we've talked a whole lot about me, Fred. What about you do you have any steamy love affairs in your background? Is Fred Cornwall your real name? How do I know anything about you? Maybe you have some kinky sexual tastes I should be concerned about?" She said all of this with a smile on her face.

"Well let's see: no, yes, all you have to do is ask, and not that I know of, if that's even relevant."

"I have to say I am a little disappointed in that last answer, Fred. Who knows, this is just a first date, it might eventually be very relevant."

"Do you have any kinky sexual tastes I should be concerned about?" I responded.

"Yes, and if I were you, I would be concerned," she said, looking at me steadily with those huge blue eyes, a faint smile on her face.

By the time dessert came I was full but I ate the stone fruit galette anyway because it was so damn good, slices of black plum on buttery puff pastry with a redcurrant glaze. Ariella ordered a calvados but I was already contemplating needing to Uber back to Hermosa so I passed on any more liquor and ordered coffee.

When the bill came, she grabbed it but I could see it was for over twelve hundred dollars. She smiled that Ariella smile at me as she pulled out a credit card and gave it to the waiter. When she signed the credit card receipt, I couldn't quite make out the signature but it wasn't Ariella Smith. In fact, there didn't seem to be an Ariella in the signature at all. "I can't thank you enough for a superb meal, Ariella. I enjoyed it," I said quite sincerely. It was rare I ate this well.

"I could probably find a way for you to thank me but we'll save that for another night perhaps." She smiled.

As we walked out of the restaurant, she took my arm. As we stood waiting at the curb for the valet to bring our cars, she turned to face me, coming close. "I really enjoyed tonight," she said. "I should, obviously, get out more. I have another trip coming up in a couple of days. I'll call you when I get back."

As the valet pulled her car up, she kissed me on the lips. It was a soft, moist, warm kiss that lit me up like an electrical current. As shaken as I was, I couldn't help but notice this woman who bought us a meal that must have cost fifteen hundred dollars with tax and tip and bragged about how much money she made, climbed into a five-year-old dusty gray Toyota Camry.

Seven
Hermosa Beach

Lindsay had a great morning on the beach playing volleyball. She aced a couple of serves and spiked a ball right in the face of Becky Messing. Fred Cornwall did not show up for the game. She was bummed. It had been weeks since he came into Hennessy's so Sunday mornings were her only chance to see him. She had to admit she was getting increasingly desperate.

To her great joy, Fred showed up at Malloy's for post-game festivities. As soon as she saw him come in, she made room at the table and grabbed an empty chair from the next table.

"Thanks, Lindsay," he acknowledged.

She noticed he looked pale and pasty faced with dark bags under his red blurry eyes.

"So, where did you drag yourself in from?"

"Oh, a late dinner last night and a lot of liquor. I can't believe I made it home."

"A client?"

"No, that girl I met in Chinatown. I think I told you about her, long dark hair, huge blue eyes, incredible body."

Lindsay was not liking the sound of this at all.

"She finally called me about three weeks after we met. She took me out to Lucques and guess what, she paid for dinner."

He said this as if he had bagged some sort of dangerous game or won a sports championship. Lindsay was determined to find out more.

"So, did you bang her?" It was something she never would have said had it not been for the two celebratory Bloody Marys she gulped down before Fred showed up.

"Lindsay, c'mon, you don't ask questions like that."

"I bet you'll talk about it with your guy friends," she snapped at him and got up to leave, in the process of which she dumped the remains of her third Bloody Mary in his lap.

For not the first time that weekend Fred ruminated on how inscrutable he found women.

Eight
Tegucigalpa, Honduras

The death of Maria Amendola prompted several prominent environmental groups to lobby for the FBI to get involved in a tragedy the government of Honduras was eager to have forgotten. At the insistence of the American ambassador, a tactical team of FBI specialists was sent to the Honduran capital to assist local authorities in the investigation of this prominent and courageous woman.

Amendola was the leader of a movement of indigenous Hondurans who were trying to stop a major hydroelectric project in the Honduran mountains. The group claimed the river to be affected by multiple dams built for the project was sacred to an indigenous group who lived in the area. The project would have a disastrous effect on wildlife and plant life throughout the watershed of the river, displacing hundreds of indigenous inhabitants.

While the Honduran government, not noted for its concerns about the environment or its indigenous inhabitants, was solidly behind the project, Maria Amendola raised the profile of the resistance and attracted international attention. All of this was creating problems with the American financial backers. Her demise was convenient for the continuation of a project destined to make certain people a great deal of money.

For Chandler Diaz, who was included in the task force dispatched to Honduras, the motive seemed clear. Of course, Honduras was a country plagued with violence. Some called Tegucigalpa the murder capital of the world. The local authorities were quick to point out that Amendola could simply have been a random one of the daily body count that piled up in the city's morgue.

Amendola was an easy target, regardless of who did the killing. While friends in the village in which she lived kept watch over her home when she was there, this murder had happened in Tegucigalpa while she was lobbying the government to stop the project. She was staying in a small hotel on the outskirts of the city. She had no bodyguards and the hotel had little security. She was found with her throat slashed in her room. The local authorities assured him it was a gang killing. There was no evidence of robbery, no reason to think the local gangs had any reason to target her. Of course, someone might have paid a gang to assassinate her and the slit throat seemed consistent with their style.

Diaz thought if he really wanted someone dead, he would probably not hire a neighborhood gang to do it. Gangs in Honduras killed sometimes for revenge, usually for power. Rarely were they used as hired killers, nor were they often used by the government, which tended to use its own security services for assassinations. Diaz thought if it was a government ministry or official who ordered the killing that is how they would have done it. Had it been one of the investors in the hydroelectric project, perhaps they would have used a professional killer. In either case finding witnesses willing to talk was going to be difficult.

Things had opened up a bit in the Singapore investigation. They discovered from a family domestic servant that Tsi had probably been molesting his son. They found his wife made two separate transfers of one hundred thousand dollars each to the same Cayman Island account. One transfer occurred about two weeks before the murder and the other about three days after. To Diaz this seemed like a hefty fee for an assassin.

On the other hand, Tsi was heavily guarded, rode in an armored limousine and moved in rarified circles. He was a difficult target. If the mother was trying to protect her son, no price would have been too high. Of course, the receiving Cayman Island account was anonymous, owned by a corporation owned by a trust with an unknown beneficiary, so it would be impossible to trace ownership or the ultimate destination of the funds.

Still, Singapore authorities were reviewing Mrs. Tsi's

communications to see if they could find evidence of her contacting the killer. While their progress was slow, he felt they were moving ahead. They could be pretty certain who was responsible for the killing and what the motive had been even though they did not have enough to allow the Singapore prosecutor to charge her yet. They did not know for sure the identity of the person who pulled the actual trigger. They did know it had been a high-level professional killer with an expensive price tag.

The Osorio killing was not progressing as well. The funds used to pay the killer undoubtedly came from an offshore bank account and were transferred into one so there was little chance of following the money. There was a strong likelihood the parties behind the killing were Venezuelan officials beyond the reach of the FBI or the U.S. Attorney's Office. That left the actual killer, who had been exceptionally clever, covered his tracks well but might still be within reach of U.S. law enforcement.

Diaz was beginning to think perhaps a trap of some kind had been set up in Osorio's hotel room to administer the poison injection. He had agents looking into the hotel cleaning crew that prepared the rooms. Anything out of the ordinary might result in a real lead. While to most investigators, the lack of progress in the one case that was within his jurisdiction where he could make an actual arrest would be frustrating, to Diaz there was a special challenge in dealing with a killer who so cleverly covered his tracks. He relished the chance to reel this one in.

Nine
Ti George's Chicken, Los Angeles

Eugene loved this place. I have to say the chicken is pretty good and they do have the best cup of coffee I've had in a restaurant. Eugene says it reminds him of Haiti where he has gone dozens of times to visit relatives. He loves chatting up the owner, George, in Creole.

For about the price of a mojito at Lucques you can get a half chicken, marinated in fruit juice and chilies, rotisserie roasted to a turn, along with a spicy coleslaw salad and fried plantains. I never object to eating at Ti Georges when Eugene suggests it.

"So, after your date, have you heard from your dream girl?" Eugene asked with a snide smile.

"Not a word and of course, I still have no way to contact her."

"So, maybe the date didn't go as well as you thought?"

"I don't know. I mean she kissed me, a kiss that completely sent me to Jupiter and back. That had to mean something, right?"

"Or nothing. You know women. They never say what they mean. They avoid confrontation, keep their real feelings to themselves or wait to express them to their girlfriends. They're never straight up with the men in their lives."

I contemplated this cynical wisdom while attacking the sweet and spicy roast chicken on my plate. Eugene is always trying to get me to go to Haiti with him. I never have any time or money to go anywhere. Haiti would not be my destination of choice but man, if the food is like this there, I may change my mind.

"Do you know anything about her friends? You know the circle she hangs with?"

"Nothing. For all I know she has no friends. All I know is that she travels a lot, wears very expensive clothes, is incredibly secretive about where she lives and her phone number. She may even use an alias. In any case, she won't tell me her last name. She seems to have a lot of money."

"Yet you tell me she drives a dusty old Camry. In L.A., who with money drives a Camry? Here people who live in walk-up rented apartments drive Mercedes. That's a car for married couples struggling to pay the mortgage and feed the kids. In this town, bank tellers drive BMWs and Audis."

"Yeah, it was pretty weird. She just paid for a fifteen-hundred-dollar meal for a virtual stranger on a first date, and she's the girl who's not even supposed to pay."

"Maybe she was just trying to impress you?"

"You haven't seen this girl. She doesn't have to struggle to impress anyone. When she walked into the restaurant every male eye and quite a few female ones followed her like she was a celebrity. Any guy would have bought her dinner. Hell, I would have paid fifteen hundred for dinner with her and I can't afford it. Plus, she really knew her wines and food. The wines she ordered were obscenely expensive but she got her money's worth. They were incredible."

"All of this sounds too strange to be real, man. I think you are just making this up. I won't believe until I actually meet her and I doubt that ever happens."

"Well, so do I. It's something that seems too good to be true so it probably is. Really, Eugene, she is real. I admit she doesn't make much sense."

"Look, friend, stop obsessing over this woman. Surely there must be someone else. Some simpleminded little cutie impressed by the corporate lawyer with the Hermosa Beach condo? You may not be a prize for a girl like this Ariella but you are not a bad catch. Have you ever tried to figure out why she singled you out for a drink and dinner?"

"Must be my unique charm. Honestly, I don't know. I guess this seems like my one chance to land a beautiful girl who I am really attracted to. We both know women don't always make a lot of sense to us and that there are ordinary guys who have ended up with incredible women, so it's possible this might actually be real. I am going to hang onto the hope until I come crashing down. If it turns out to be an illusion, I'll have to deal with the disappointment. It won't be the first time and somehow I'll survive."

"I admire you, my friend. I think in your shoes I would run away and hide. The girl sounds like trouble but hey, in the end she may be worth it."

We sat for a while and sipped the delicious coffee before going our separate ways.

Ten
New York City

Helen Beckworth called down to the doorman to have a taxi waiting for her when she came down from her forty-seventh-floor co-op. She rarely left the five-thousand-one-hundred-square-foot home which took up an entire floor of her high-rise building and had a special keyed elevator.

The building had a doorman and front desk receptionist on duty twenty-four hours, seven days a week. Her maid did most of her shopping for her. She was the heiress to a fortune built originally on New England textile mills and cannily converted into Manhattan real estate during the depression. Her lawyers told her several years ago it was worth over six hundred million dollars with a steady and growing income from rents. Now sixty-four, she lived alone, her fortune-hunting bounder of a husband having fortunately died years ago. She abhorred her two children whose only interest in their mother seemed to relate to her money. She had since cut off their allowances and now not seen Abbie or James in over two years.

The occasion for her rare venture into the outer world was to have lunch with old friend, Millicent Gardner. Millie had been her college roommate at Wellesley, lived in New York for more than twenty years, now lived in Palm Beach with her husband. Helen relished the chance to see her. She took the secure elevator down to where William, the doorman, had a cab waiting. She told the driver to take her to the Russian Tea Room on Fifty-Seventh.

When she got there, Millie was already there and had a table. They hugged and sat down to study the menu. They ordered a pot of Darjeeling, a caviar sampler to share, Chicken Kiev for Millie and grilled salmon for Helen. When the tea came, they each took a cup from the pot and Millie started talking about her grandchildren in Connecticut.

Helen noticed the tea seemed somewhat bitter and looked around for a waitress to send the pot back. As she scanned the dining room, she felt her muscles begin to tighten and her heart felt strange, speeding up and slowing down randomly. In a panic she looked over at Millie to see her drooling and gasping for air.

Helen felt her heart stop beating, tremble then speed up at an insane rate. Millie looked like her eyes were about to pop out of her head. By now waiters and other customers were all around them. Helen felt her heart seize up in a sharp contraction and fell out of her chair.

Someone called 911. By now both women were on the floor, seemingly having seizures. By the time the paramedics arrived both women were inert on the floor, their eyes and mouths frozen open.

Police officers arrived and confiscated the pot of tea and remains of the caviar sampler. The restaurant was closed. A homicide detective interviewed all of the customers and staff before they were released, taking names, addresses, phone numbers. A single old woman having a public heart attack might not have been suspicious but two older women having identical symptoms after sharing a pot of tea and plate of food was very suspicious.

After the bodies were taken away, an NYPD detective was sent to notify next of kin, both of whom lived in the city.

Abigail Beckworth answered the door when Detective Becky Haden knocked on the door of her one-room flat in Brooklyn Heights. Abbie Beckworth was an attractive twenty-four-year-old with large green eyes and a bottle-blonde perm. Haden thought she and her apartment looked cheap for a daughter of a filthy rich widow.

"I am very sorry to tell you that your mother passed away today under unusual circumstances."

Abbie's eyes widened a bit.

"What do you mean unusual circumstances?"

"She and a friend were lunching at the Russian Tea Room and

both had seemingly identical heart attacks."

The daughter seemed surprisingly calm at the news, glancing at Detective Haden expressionlessly.

"Do you mind if I ask you a few questions?"

"Of course not."

"Pardon me if I say you seem rather calm at the news. Were you and your mother not on good terms?"

"I hadn't spoken to my mother for over two years. She completely cut me and my brother off, no allowance, no gifts, not even a birthday card. She couldn't stand us. So no, I would have to say we were not on good terms."

"Do you know if you stand to inherit any part of your mother's fortune?"

"That's a good question. I have no idea what sort of will she had. If I had to bet, I would say that James and I don't get a penny, but I really don't know."

"Where were you between twelve-fifteen and one-thirty this afternoon?"

"That's easy. I was at an AA meeting in the basement meeting room of Saint Patrick's parish hall. There must have been at least fifteen other people there, I'm sure they would all vouch for me. The meeting went from twelve noon to two-thirty P.M. I was there for the whole thing, as usual."

"I tried to call your brother earlier. Do you have any idea where I can reach him?"

"Yeah, he's in Montreal. He works for a metal importer. He goes there a lot. I'll give you his hotel name and number."

Millie Gardner's husband and daughter received calls. Both seemed deeply upset by the news.

James Beckworth was finally contacted at his Montreal hotel and had the same calm, chilly reaction as his sister. He too claimed to know nothing about his mother's estate.

So, thought Becky Haden several days later as she reviewed the case file, *Millie Gardner and her husband were retirees living on a modest income with a married daughter who seemed on very good terms with her mother. Helen Beckworth, on the other hand, was worth hundreds of millions of dollars and had two children who seemed to hate her guts. Her two children, the prime suspects if this was indeed murder, had ironclad alibies that only got better upon investigation. Yet two women died simultaneously with identical symptoms, it had to be murder and somehow the Beckworth children were the only people who might gain from the death of their mother, if only out of revenge for her cutting them off from a vast fortune.*

This notion was reinforced when it was discovered Helen Beckworth had left no will or trust. This seemed very strange for such an affluent individual. Her lawyer indicated he had drawn up a will which left her entire fortune to a variety of charities and specifically disinherited her two children. However, as far as he knew, it had never been signed. Under New York law, if an individual died without a will or trust, "intestate" as the lawyers called it, the estate went to the next of kin. In this case split evenly between James and Abigail Beckworth.

As Haden pondered the possibilities, the toxicology report from the autopsy became available. None of the poisons the scan routinely tested for had shown up in the bodies of either woman.

Eleven
Downtown Los Angeles.

It had been three and a half weeks since dinner at Lucques. I was disappointed not to hear from Ariella and yeah, maybe a little confused. I thought the date went well. The way she talked and that kiss, maybe it was the start of something. Since then not a word and, of course, she never gave me any contact information on her so it was almost as if the whole encounter had been a fantasy. As I thought about it, I began to get mad. She had been so damn flippant when I complained about not having her contact information, like I could not be trusted to not violate her sacred privacy. It was very strange and frustrating because I liked her a lot. It wasn't just that she was the most attractive woman I ever dated. Hell, she was one of the most attractive women I had ever even seen. She was suave, cool and smart. She was elegant and confident. I hadn't met many guys as cocky as she was and never a woman. I wanted to know more about her. I wanted to know everything about her like a mystery that just has to be solved.

So, when the receptionist at the office told me there was an Ariella on the phone for me, almost a month after we had last connected, my first reaction was annoyance, but I took the call.

"Hey Fred," said the light, musical voice on the other end. "How are you?"

"Relieved that you're still alive. I just assumed the worst," I answered.

She laughed.

"I'm better than just alive, Fred. I apologize that it's been so long but I've been very busy and you know how fast time goes when you're engaged, right? I have missed you and thought about you, Fred."

"Really?"

"Yeah, maybe I can make things up to you by taking you to a concert Friday night, at the Wiltern theatre? It's a group called *Nueva Manteca*. You like Latin jazz, don't you, Fred?"

"Well, yeah. Actually, I think I've heard of that group. Aren't the musicians mostly Dutch?"

"That's the group. I just got back from Panama and it's exactly the music I want to hear. What about it, Fred?"

"Well, yeah," I said, the anger melting away as I spoke. "Do you want to have dinner or something?"

"Maybe after the concert we can go to a bar I know nearby, get some drinks and bar food?"

"Sounds like a plan. Do you need me to get the tickets?"

"I already have them, seventh row center. You just need to show up. We can meet at the front entrance at seven forty-five."

"Okay, see you then," I said, any anger I may have felt having completely slipped away.

"I'm looking forward to it," she said, then hung up.

I wasn't sure what to make of the invitation coming as it did after so many weeks of silence from her. I realized I was completely at her beck and call. She was in total control of whatever it was we seemed to be having, not sure I could call it a "relationship." In the end, what did I have to lose? I had no girlfriend and no one else I was even interested in. Plus, I hadn't invested a dime in this girl, she paid for everything. So, I guess I could play along and see where this went even if it ended up not going anywhere. Like I said, I had nothing to lose.

Twelve
New York City

Detective Becky Haden had no objection to working with the FBI Special Homicide Unit on the Beckworth/Gardner deaths. She liked Special Agent Chandler Diaz, a tall, light-skinned Black man with green eyes and a quiet, confident demeanor. Diaz suggested they use the FBI labs to run some special toxicology tests.

The first battery of tests came back negative. Diaz ordered a second round of tests to include less common poisons. This test detected high levels of batrachotoxin in the bodies of both women.

"It's a poison derived from glands in the golden dart frog," said Diaz. "The frog is native to Central America. Natives use the poison to tip darts for blowguns. It's not going to be easy to trace something like this. Unfortunately, the Tea Room has no security cameras that might let us see if anyone tampered with the tea pot brought to their table."

"So where do we go from here?" asked Haden.

"The logical suspects are the two children. We don't know for sure they didn't know their mother had no will. Their alibis are convenient but they could easily have paid someone to do the killing. I suggest we focus on them because they have the most likely motive. They clearly hated their mother whether they expected to get anything from her estate or not. We need to see if either of them had a major financial transaction recently, one that could have been used to pay a hired killer. We try to trace the money to see where it leads."

A routine check of financial records revealed that James Beckworth had recently refinanced his Brooklyn condominium. The proceeds of the refinance, almost fifty thousand dollars, appeared to have been transferred out of his bank account to a Cayman Island anonymous account that was untraceable, owned by a Panamanian corporation that was owned by a trust, the trustee of which was a lawyer located in Panama City, Panama. "Let's go talk to Mister Beckworth," said Diaz.

James Beckworth lived in a heavily gentrified section of Brooklyn Heights. The 1890s-era four-story red brick building he lived in had probably once been a factory and was now divided into loft-style condominiums. Beckworth's unit was a spacious third-floor studio with bathroom and kitchen tucked away discreetly in a corner. The floors were maple hardwood, and heating and air conditioning ducts ran openly overhead. Beckworth was a tall, slender man in his early thirties with cold blue eyes, pale skin afflicted with mild acne and dirty blond hair.

He greeted them without surprise and seemed preternaturally calm. "You're telling me my mother was murdered?" he asked.

"There is no question she was poisoned. We found traces of poison in the pot of tea," said Diaz. "We're checking every lead right now."

"Well, you know I was in Canada, right? There are multiple witnesses to my presence in Montreal, so I couldn't possibly have done it."

"We've checked out your alibi and we know it's good. We have some questions about the money you transferred out of your account last month into a numbered Cayman Islands account. It was over forty-eight thousand dollars. Where did it go and why?" asked Haden.

"That's easy. I have a gambling problem. I owed a lot of money and I was getting scared. I was able to refi the condo and pull out some cash. The money went to an anonymous account because the gambling was illegal, a high-stakes poker game in Manhattan run by some not very nice people. That's where they directed me to send the money. I'm going to get help for my problem. I never want to be in this position again. Did you think I paid somebody to off old Mom?"

"That thought had occurred to us, yes," said Diaz. "Is there anyone who can confirm your money went to a gambling debt?"

"Seems pretty unlikely any of the folks I dealt with would talk to

41

the FBI about collecting illegal gambling debts. My sister knew about my problems, no else did."

"Did you know your mother's death would result in you inheriting a fortune?" asked Haden.

Beckworth laughed. "That's the irony. You think you have the perfect motive but I always assumed she disinherited us years ago. She hated us. Can you imagine a mother without a shred of affection for her own children? I admit, I hated her. I haven't talked to her in years. I got a decent job, support myself and never dreamed I would inherit a dime. If I knew I was coming into big money would I have taken on debt to pay my gambling debts? That would have been foolish."

"Well then," asked Haden, "who else would have had a motive to kill your mother?"

"Ha, ha, how would I know? I know nothing of my mother's life over the last few years. I can say she was an unpleasant, malevolent woman who might certainly have made enemies, almost certainly did have enemies. Anyway, wasn't some friend of hers killed as well? Why are you assuming it was Mother who was the target? Couldn't it have been the other woman?"

As they walked back to the car Diaz observed, "I think he is our guy. There is no way we can disprove his claim he paid off a gambling debt any more than he can prove that's what he did. I think that money went to pay a hired killer. He was just a little too calm and prepared for our questions."

"A hired killer would be worth almost fifty grand?" asked Haden.

"More. My guess is that the money was a down payment on the job and the killer expects the balance now that the job is done. Beckworth and his sister will soon have their hands on a great deal of money, more than enough to complete payment. It may seem like a lot of money but whoever pulled this off left no trace. They were very good. They used a rare form of poison they probably bought from a source in Central America or even crafted themselves that will be hard to trace. Killers like that are pricey. For James and his sister, it was a good investment. I would focus on trying to find out how they found out about there being no will, whether or not they knew that their mother had a will prepared disinheriting them she hadn't signed yet. We will keep watch on James' accounts to see if there is a second major payment going out. Perhaps we can put a hold on it if we can get a court order."

Thirteen
Wiltern Theater, Los Angeles

Naturally, I got there early. I stood outside the front doors of the theater on Wilshire like a kid waiting for his mom to pick him up. Yeah, I was probably a little too eager and trying hard not to show it. It was over four weeks since our dinner at Lucques and I was puzzled about what was really going on between us. I really liked the girl but I found this weird distance she preserved between us to be unsettling. I wanted an actual relationship, you know, seeing each other every week, talking on the phone, maybe even spending the night together at one of our respective places. The fact is I had no idea where she lived, other than her vague reference to San Pedro. She never asked for my address or home phone number.

When she finally showed up, Ariella was dressed all in black in a sleeveless silk sort of shirt dress that was tight around the waist, with a black wrap around her shoulders that looked like cashmere. This was a girl who didn't wear a lot of makeup, a little rouge, pale pink lipstick and just a touch of eyeliner. Being so beautiful she didn't need much. Her long black hair hung loose, all the way to her shoulder blades with just the hint of a curl. Ariella looked genuinely pleased to see me which frankly I just found puzzling. Everything about her was puzzling.

"Hey Fred," she said with a smile, giving me a little hug and a peck on the cheek, taking my arm as we went into the theater.

The Wiltern occupies the bottom floors of a jade-green Art Deco building at the corner of Wilshire and 6th Street. It was built in 1931 and the interior is pretty much original with a huge plaster sun shape on the ceiling, golden columns, decorative tiles, patterned grill work, amazing stuff. I had been there a few years before for a Diana Krall concert.

As Ariella said the seats were seventh row center, just far enough away from the music to not be overwhelmed with the sound but close enough to see the sweat on the musicians' brows.

"What have you been up to?" I asked as we sat there waiting for the concert to begin.

"Busy, Fred. Look, I'm sorry I've been out of touch so much. I've been doing a lot of traveling. Don't take it personally. When I'm on the road, I don't have a lot of time to make contact and keep in touch. That's just something you may have to accept."

She took my hand and squeezed it and kept it there. I noticed her hands were perfectly manicured but they were large for a woman's hands and her grip was strong.

The musicians came out on stage and began warming up. There was a trumpet player, saxophone, trombone, stand-up bass, piano, drummer and *conguero*. All of them, except for the conga player, were white Europeans, mostly Dutch, but the music was vividly Latin with a complex beat. They started with a Latin version of the theme from *The Godfather*, horns combining to carry the rhythm, piano playing a counter rhythm and drums and congas providing a hard driving beat. Ariella sat back, her hand in mine, obviously enjoying the music. They followed up with a version of Miles Davis' "All Blues," then some original compositions with a decidedly Caribbean flare. The time flew by. After an hour and a half of uninterrupted music the band took their bows, did an encore, and a second encore, after which the house lights went on.

"What did you think?" asked Ariella.

"Loved it," I said sincerely.

It was definitely the sort of music I love and which, in a place like L.A., a jazz desert despite the image created by the film *La La Land*, can be hard to come by.

"Let's go get a drink. There's that bar I told you about just around the corner on Sixth."

We left the theater and walked silently arm in arm, crossing Wilshire and walking the deserted street. The place she was talking about was a little hole in the wall called Max's. It was dark inside and mostly empty. The place was a narrow hallway with wood paneling halfway up the walls, a dusty ceiling fan, tile floor and an old mahogany bar toward the back. There were rickety wood tables spread out in the front and back of the room and dark wooden booths across from the bar. We grabbed a booth. A waitress, middle aged, bottle blonde, tired looking, took our order. Ariella had a Calvados. I had a bourbon and soda.

"Sometimes when I'm in Panama I drive into Panama City. There are a couple of bars there that always have music and sometimes it's not bad, small Latin jazz combos. It can be fun. Seems like Panama City has something for everyone."

"So why Panama? What do you do when you're there?"

"My house is pretty much far from civilization. It's surrounded by jungle. There are monkeys in the trees some days, exotic birds, iguanas. It's wild and peaceful at the same time, if that makes any sense. If I really want some action, I can drive the two hours to Panama City."

"Action? What sort of action?"

"Fred, I'm not sure I know you well enough to discuss my secret vices. That's something we're going to have to work on."

"You'll get no argument from me on that," I said, not really knowing what we were talking about.

"When I'm there, I just relax, read, swim in the pool, walk in the jungle, get no cell service, ignore the news and basically just depart from reality for a while. I'm usually there after a very stressful trip. I use the peacefulness and isolation to unwind"

"So why live in L.A. at all?"

"Because I need a base with good communications. A lot of my business is done over the internet and I need a good connection. Plus, it's easy to be anonymous in a place as big as L.A. and, of course, it's still my hometown."

"Why is it important to be anonymous?" I asked, genuinely puzzled.

"It's just me. I'm a very private person, or haven't you figured that out yet?" She said.

I laughed and she took my hand across the table.

"There's a hotel just down the street. Are you ready for some playtime?"

"Absolutely," I said, grinning but shocked.

She paid the bill and we walked hand in hand down Wilshire to the Normandie Hotel, a grim-looking old brick building with a modern interior. She quickly booked a room on the fourth floor. It was a typically anonymous hotel room: beige walls, textured carpet, grey-finished king bed with matching night stands and a couple of bland abstract prints on the wall.

She quickly stripped to a black bra and black thong panties. I shed my clothes as fast as I could. She stepped toward me, kissed me hard on the lips, slipped her head down to my neck and bit me so hard she drew blood.

I woke up the next morning, a Saturday, to find her gone. A note on the pillow next to me, written in a large and florid hand. *Had a wonderful evening, needed to make an early meeting. The hotel bill is taken care of. I'll talk to you soon, this time I promise it won't be so long. Love, Ariella.*

There was blood on the sheets next to me and my face felt as if it had been caught in a vice. I looked in the mirror over the dresser and saw the entire right side of my face was purple with bruises.

Fourteen
Hermosa Beach

Once again Fred did not turn up for volleyball on Sunday. Lindsay reflected this was becoming a habit lately for Fred. Sundays were the only time for Lindsay to make contact and she badly needed the opportunity to let him know she was interested, as subtly as possible, of course. At Patrick Molloy's, as she sat at the table with the rest of the crew, sweaty and tired, cradling a large Bloody Mary in her hand, Fred came through the door and headed for the table. She quickly made room for him next to her and he grabbed the only empty seat.

Lindsay apologized weeks before for spilling her drink on Fred as she stormed out of the restaurant after asking him if he had sex with this mystery woman he kept talking about. She was still nervous around him, realized she needed to dial down her emotions when she talked to him or risk making a fool of herself. As he turned to say hello, she saw that the entire right side of his face was dark purple with bruises and his right eye was black with bruising.

"My god, Fred, I hope the other guy looks worse than you."

"Oh, yeah, it was no big deal, just a kind of, well, a misunderstanding but it's all good."

"What happened, Fred?" she asked hoping to evoke not only a conversation with him, but also details about his life about which she knew little.

"Really nothing, no big deal."

"Did it have anything to do with that mystery girl you've been dating?"

"Sort of, but I wouldn't say we've been dating. I don't even know her last name or where she lives. Hell, I don't even have her phone number."

"Did she slap you around, Fred?" asked Lindsay, laughing.

Fred blushed so that the rest of his face almost matched the bruises.

My god, thought Lindsay, *she did slap him around.*

"Like I say it was nothing, but I did see a really good Latin jazz group, though, at the Wiltern. Great concert," he added, trying obviously to change the subject

"You went with mystery girl?"

"Yeah, it was her idea but the concert was really good."

"You got fresh with her and she knocked you around?" asked Lindsay hopefully.

"Not exactly, no. I'm not that kind of aggressive guy."

"Some guy tried to cut in on you and you tangled?"

"No, not what happened."

"Maybe you guys had some kind of kinky sex and you got the worst of it?" Again, Fred's scarlet face got more scarlet.

"Uhh, I'm going to go use the restroom okay, I'll be back," he said as he scooted back his chair and stumbled off toward the back of the restaurant. He never did come back. Lindsay was left to wonder just what Fred had gotten himself into and just what kind of dude Fred really was. She had to admit though that, far from being a turn off, this actually made Fred even more interesting.

Fifteen
Brooklyn Heights

There was an e-mail on James Beckworth's phone from a "medusa199." *Services have been rendered,* it read. *Final payment is due immediately.* Beckworth was irritated. He saw no reason to pay.

His response read, *You botched the job by creating collateral damage which has directed suspicion at my sister and myself. Be satisfied with what you have received. You will get no more.*

Beckworth was annoyed that his mother's death, which should have looked like a heart attack instead, because of the identical demise of Millie Gardner at the exact same moment, looked suspicious and the clever FBI guy ordered tests that detected the poison. Naturally, he and his sister looked like ideal suspects even with ironclad alibis, or maybe especially because they had iron clad alibis.

Months ago, their mother's maid alerted them to the existence of a new will disinheriting them both. She was handsomely rewarded for purloining it and Mother had forgotten all about it, as these days she was likely to do. The FBI, of course, tracked down his condo refi and his payment into an anonymous Cayman account. It was an investigation which would not have happened if his mother died alone. He still owed "medusa199" over one-hundred-and-fifty-thousand dollars, but if he paid the FBI would know about it and be all over him. Forty-eight-thousand dollars was a lot of money to pay for the death of a doddering old lady, two hundred thousand was absurd, highway robbery. "Medusa199" should be happy with his payday and let it go before they all got caught. A new e-mail from "medusa199" popped up on his phone: *Pay within twenty-four hours or accept the consequences.* Well, James would avoid Russian Tea Rooms. He decided other than that there did not seem to be any reason for concern from "medusa199."

James was already planning how to spend his mother's money. His first act would be to quit his job as a representative for a metal wholesaler and importer. He would sell his condo and buy a townhouse in Manhattan. His mother's flat would be sold. Neither he nor Abbie could abide living in it. They would split the proceeds. Time in the Caribbean would be nice. Maybe he would buy a house on Saint Bart's and split his time between Manhattan and the islands. Maybe he would buy a small yacht and hop from island to island. Also, time in Paris might be nice and he could afford a small flat there as well. The possibilities, like his mother's fortune, now his fortune, seemed endless.

The next day, as he was cruising the internet on his laptop at his kitchen table with a cup of black coffee, another e-mail from "medusa199" popped up on his screen. *Time's up, James. You have made a life-changing mistake.*

Sixteen
Washington D.C.

Diaz sat at his desk in FBI headquarters reviewing his case files. The Osorio case was beginning to focus somewhat.

Osorio had gone down in the elevator to the lobby with a single FBI escort and a maid's cart with two maids. It was not impossible Osorio was pricked with a poison-loaded needle in the elevator. The agent did not remember the faces of the two maids but they had gotten a list of all housekeeping personnel on duty at that hour and an agent on Diaz's team was interviewing everyone. So far, no one remembered going down in the elevator with Osorio and the agent. Eventually they would find the maids who went down with them.

The Singapore case was in stasis. The authorities there brought in Mrs. Tsi for an interview, but she steadfastly denied her late husband molested their son, claiming it was just malicious gossip. She explained away the money transfers as payments to a cousin who was in financial difficulty with real estate deals in Taiwan. The numbered Cayman Island accounts were to hide the money from her creditors. She offered the name of the cousin and Singapore police were in the process of locating and interviewing her.

As for the Amendola case, Honduran authorities located a witness who recalled seeing a dark-haired woman in a rustic cotton skirt and blouse whose face was covered by a black mantilla in the vicinity of the entrance to Amendola's hotel. The witness assumed because of her dress the woman was indigenous who might be a friend or associate. This alone was not much but it opened up some other lines of inquiry.

Perhaps Amendola was killed as a result of a fissure in the political movement opposing the project? Diaz did not think the killer was a woman, the murder was too brutal and would have required considerable strength. Besides, in a machismo society like Honduras, killing was a man's job. This mysterious woman would have been one of the last people to see the victim alive. They needed to make every attempt to locate her. Diaz assumed the responsible party was either the Honduran authorities or the American backers of the project. The financing was provided by a hedge fund called Atrios Financial who had already committed over eighty million dollars. A review of their finances might reveal some unaccounted-for payments that could be traced to a killer. The other suspect, the Honduran National Power Authority or ANP, was a government agency that would have used the national police or the military to do the killing. If it was ANP that orchestrated the assassination, it might prove impossible to trace but perhaps there was a way to scrutinize their finances without raising too much suspicion within the Honduran government.

Diaz considered the Beckworth case all but solved. The suspects were obvious: Abbie and James Beckworth had strong motivation to eliminate their mother. The fact they both had such ironclad alibis actually made Diaz even more convinced they set up the murder. James refinanced his condominium in order to hire a killer to do the actual killing. Diaz was convinced that the initial payment was not the full amount being paid to the killer. He had an alert on James' and Abbie's accounts to trace the final payment. James had already filed to have himself named as executor of his mother's estate and received a court order allowing him access to the estate's assets so the money was available. The killer was no doubt expecting to get paid very soon. The second payment might lead them to the actual killer, but even if it did not it was strong circumstantial evidence the siblings were behind the crime. As he was thinking about the case, he received a phone call from Detective Haden in New York. They had finally gotten a warrant to search James and Abbie's apartments. There had been so little evidence they had problems convincing a judge to issue a warrant. Now that they had one, they were on their way to James' condo. Perhaps his laptop or phone might provide clues to his contacts with the hired killer. Haden promised to call Diaz as soon as they were through.

Seventeen
Hermosa Beach

The whole encounter with Lindsay made me wonder, was I ashamed of what happened with Ariella? Was I weird? I guess I didn't realize what I wanted so badly or at least wouldn't admit to myself. It was now so clear why my other relationships hadn't been satisfying sexually, but how did Ariella know?

"It's just a game," she said at first. "Just play, relax, let yourself go and get into it."

Really, it wasn't hard, it was what I wanted, just to let go, let her take charge. The pain, well, the pain was like joy, it was bliss. I had never known or never let myself realize. It's true I had fantasies I never admitted to anyone. That should have told me everything I needed to know about my desires but I wouldn't let myself think about it. Was I ashamed? Yes, yes, I was.

I just wanted to be like everyone else, to blend in. I loved the volleyball group because I was just one of the guys, not special, part of a friendly, funny group that wanted to have fun. Showing up with the bruises was a mistake. That damn Lindsay just couldn't keep her mouth shut about it. I guess I should have lied and said I got into a fight. I was caught off guard. I am just not a natural liar. I know it's probably a career disadvantage for a lawyer but when pressed I usually blurt out the truth.

The hard part was accepting who I am or who I must be given the experience with Ariella. I was weird, I wasn't like everybody else. I might not be a liar, I was living the ultimate lie, pretending to be someone I wanted to be but was not. Now Ariella, she didn't seem to care much about being like everybody else. She was beautiful, rich, and seemed to do whatever she wanted. Even the way she moved was so confident, head held high, gliding along on those ever-present high heels, knowing every time she walked into a room all eyes were on her and not giving a damn what they think. I envied that self-confidence but I could never be that way myself.

The thought that I was different, odd, maybe even a sort of pervert: that bothered me a lot. I didn't know what to do with it. For years I had kept the box firmly closed and now this encounter with Ariella opened it. This wasn't just a game. It was something I didn't want to do but couldn't help doing.

Should I stop seeing Ariella? It was a strange relationship in which she was firmly in control. It did not appear to be going anywhere. I still didn't know her last name, phone number or where she lived. I knew nothing of her friends, her social life, her interests, other than jazz. Realistically I was going to have a hard time keeping up with her if the relationship ever heated up. If I let her go, maybe I could put the lid back on the box, go back to my dull, unsatisfying "normal" life that, after all, was not so bad. A life with Ariella in it was just full of truths that were too uncomfortable to deal with.

It was a Sunday afternoon and I was at home in my Hermosa condo. When the phone rang. I was surprised. My clients have my office number which I can check periodically using my cell phone but I don't give them my cell number. After all, I'm not a criminal attorney and I don't have to worry about bailing clients out on a weekend. Maybe it was Eugene wanting to set up a lunch next week. When I answered, a familiar melodious voice came on the line. "Hey Fred, how are you?"

"Ariella, I didn't know you had my cell number."

"I did some digging around and found it. I'm pretty good at finding things. Is that a problem?"

"No, of course not. I'm glad you called. How are you?"

"Wonderful, Fred. I was wondering if you would like to hang out at my place next weekend? You know, just chill, watch a movie, maybe pick up where we left off last time? Sound good?"

"Sounds great. Let me have your address and when you want me there and it's a date."

"You'll never find my place, Fred. It's not a conventional house or condo, you can't get into the garage without a remote. You don't want to park on the street. Besides you can only get in to the living area through the garage. I'll pick you up at your place about six thirty on Friday. That will give us Friday and Saturday nights. I'll bring you back Sunday."

"Okay, let me give you my address in Hermosa."

"No problem, Fred, I've already got it. See you Friday."

Eighteen
Brooklyn Heights

Becky Haden pulled up to James Beckworth's loft, warrant in hand. She had four other detectives and a uniformed officer with her. No one answered the buzzer when they rang but they got another tenant to buzz them into the building. No one answered the door to James' unit when they knocked. They jimmied the lock and entered.

The condo seemed empty. They swept the place looking for his laptop and any paperwork he might have. The loft was essentially a large room used as a seating area, dining room and kitchen. The separate bedroom and bathroom were on the far side of the unit from the entrance. They fanned out to search. Haden was examining the books on James' shelf when an officer yelled out, "Over here!" It came from the bedroom. Haden trotted over along with the other detectives.

On the bed was James Beckworth with a bullet hole in his forehead. He was in his underwear, hands at his sides, lying peacefully. "Call CSI," said Haden. "Suddenly, we are now searching a crime scene. See if you can find his laptop anywhere."

They could find neither his laptop nor his cell phone. Haden thought for a moment, then called the precinct. "Have the closest unit check the apartment of Abbie Beckworth," she said and gave them the address.

She then put a call into Diaz and told him what they found.

"I'm going to bet you find a second body in Abbie Beckworth's apartment," he said.

Within twenty minutes his guess was confirmed. Abbie

Beckworth was found shot in the head at her kitchen table. There was no sign of her cell phone or computer.

The CSI unit that arrived at James' condo found no prints of any kind anywhere. The place had been swept clean. The M.E. who examined the body said it looked like he had been shot with a nine-millimeter hand gun but deferred to ballistics analysis, assuming they found a bullet. "This was one clean, sweet professional job," opined the CSI supervisor on the scene. "This guy was a real pro."

The verdict on Abbie's death was similar. No prints, no murder weapon, probably a nine-millimeter. No one at either building remembered seeing anyone and there was no evidence at either site of forced entry.

"My guess," said Diaz over the phone after Haden conveyed all of this to him, "is they welshed on paying our killer and this was payback. We never saw any action from either of their bank accounts or from the estate. Our killer got stiffed. Instead of solving Helen Beckworth and Millie Gardner's murders, we now have two more to add to the tally."

Nineteen
Downtown Los Angeles

Eugene and I were back at Phillippe's for lunch. I had the usual lamb dip and Eugene the pork. It was crowded so after we got our sandwiches at the counter, we took them upstairs where there were individual rooms with tables. The story was that this floor had originally been a bordello. I was not sure how true that was, but I knew Phillippe's had been here since 1951 and originally opened in another location in 1908. They claimed to have invented the French Dip sandwich, a claim shared by several other establishments, but whoever was first, Phillippe's did it as well as anyone.

Eugene slathered his pork dip in their proprietary brown mustard and dug into his macaroni salad. "So, you are finally going to see this girl's apartment?" he asked between bites.

"I guess so, she was pretty adamant that I could never find it on my own and she had to pick me up and take me there."

"Maybe she will blindfold you on the way?"

"It wouldn't surprise me. Seeing her place should tell me a lot about her. Maybe she won't be such a mystery after we've spent a weekend together at her place."

"Your bruise is healing up nicely. You never did tell me how you got it."

"Well, I have to have a few secrets even from you, right?"

"If it wasn't a fight then I am going to assume you got it from the girl."

"Assume all you want. It just wasn't a big deal and I am getting tired of people asking me about it."

"Have you had sex with her yet?"

"You're not supposed to talk about things like that. It makes her sound like a slut and me like a jerk."

"So, the answer is 'no?'"

"No, the answer is 'yes,' sort of."

"I wasn't aware there was a way to 'sort of' have sex."

"Why don't we talk about your love life?"

"Because I don't have one and even if I did, yours is a lot more interesting, particularly lately. Now, about that bruise?"

"Eugene, have you ever discovered something about or admitted something about yourself that you find troubling?"

"Probably, but go on."

"It's just that all of this thing with Ariella is getting complicated. I always dreamed of having a beautiful girlfriend, right? This whole relationship is weird and it's getting weirder. I can't get over the fact she has kept so much about herself secret, her last name, her number, her address, what she does for a living. I only see her when she wants to see me and sometimes it's not for weeks. I have no idea if there is someone else, if she's married, who her friends are. It's just a really strange relationship. Yes, the sex has been unusual too, but I like it."

"Look man, next weekend you'll know where she lives. You'll spend the whole weekend together and you can ask lots of questions. If she were married or living with someone, she wouldn't ask you over to her house, would she?"

"Are you actually being encouraging?"

"It's weird, isn't it? Man, I can see you are all torn up about this girl. I hate to see you this way. Hang in there and see where it goes. Look if it gets too weird you can always book out of the whole thing. If you do, you won't be any worse off than before you met her, will you?"

Twenty
New York City

Jonathon Parsons, founder and CEO of the health care technology company Apollo Health, took a call from a Jesse Blake. Blake represented Talisman Management which just purchased almost ten percent of Apollo Health's stock. The phone conversation had not been comforting to Parsons. Blake talked about issues with Apollo Health's profitability, the recently sinking stock price, and that other investors were also not happy. Apollo Health was a profitable company. It produced, in a good year, almost a billion dollars in gross revenue. It was true the company's overhead was too high and employee turnover was not ideal.

Parsons had a reputation of carousing with his employees and perhaps being too preoccupied with his sailing competitions and his racing sailboat. Blake raised these concerns, indicating he would be heading up a committee of shareholders who would be seeking responses from management on all these issues expecting a plan for remedial action to increase profits and shore up the stock price.

At the end of the conversation Blake told Parsons, "Don't worry, I've told my PR people to stand down, for now."

After this disturbing conversation Parsons did some research about Talisman Management. He discovered Talisman Management was controlled by Paul Voca, a notorious investor whose routine was to acquire controlling interests in corporations, displacing management, stripping the assets from the company, selling them off piecemeal or slicing the overhead to improve profits increasing stock prices before turning over the stock at a profit. In either case, the key was displacing existing management and taking control of the company. Voca often accomplished this through nefarious means. He was known to have hired private investigators to dig up dirt on top company executives.

In the next few weeks, a letter circulated to Apollo Health shareholders harshly criticizing the management of the company. The letter asserted the company was overstaffed, needed to cut payroll, that overhead was too high and a cost austerity program needed to be implemented. The letter criticized Parsons for being too obsessed with his sailboat racing. It described his sailing team as a "drinking team with a sailing problem." It accused him of having too fraternal a relationship with company employees. The letter cited the various parties and celebrations he hosted for employees. These included drinking games with employees and midnight swims on company retreats.

Parsons responded by sending out his own letter to shareholders pledging to cut overhead by fifteen percent including staffing cuts and decreased perquisites for upper management. He hoped that might stymie Talisman from convincing shareholders they needed a change in management.

Blake eventually met with the board of directors in a private meeting to which Parsons was not invited. Parsons heard he had been heavily criticized by Blake for his personal behavior, lack of attention to Apollo Health's falling stock prices, high overhead and for slack morale at company headquarters. The board took no action in response to Blake's complaints. Since Parsons was now furiously working to reduce the company's overhead by laying off several hundred employees and cutting a number of experimental programs, he felt perhaps he was safe for now.

About a month after he met with the board of directors Blake invited Parsons for dinner. That night he explained to Parsons that Talisman decided to buy Apollo Health and go private with it. An offer was being prepared for all shareholders. Blake explained to Parsons that while, of course, they would want to install their own management, he would still be involved with the company as a consultant.

Shortly thereafter, while Parsons was preparing to fight the takeover attempt by Talisman, Blake called him. "Our private investigator went through your divorce file," he told Parsons. "It seems your wife filed an affidavit that you molested your daughter. I would imagine that's not something you want released to the press is it?"

The affidavit was filed during a bitter fight about child custody. His ex-wife's attorney urged her to file it and it had been a deciding factor in her gaining primary custody of their two children, limiting him to supervised visits. The allegations were untrue. He cheated on his wife and she was deeply angry.

They had since reconciled and developed a cooperative, even friendly relationship. He now shared custody with his ex-wife, taking the children on weekends and holidays. Parsons knew the affidavit would be fatal to any attempt to fight off the takeover.

"If you resign as CEO," said Blake "We'll see that the affidavit never comes to light and we'll provide you with a generous severance package."

Parsons asked for a few days to make up his mind. He immediately dialed his lawyer and explained the situation.

"There really isn't much I can do," said the lawyer. "The information they have is part of a court file. Its use is privileged as far as defamation is concerned, which means you have no recourse for them using it. Besides, they aren't making the allegation in the affidavit, your ex-wife is. Even if there were defamation, she would be the one defaming you. They aren't doing anything that would allow you to sue to stop them."

"Even though what the affidavit says is a lie and my ex would admit it wasn't true?"

"You might try a public relations specialist. I could recommend one but once an accusation like this is out, you will be tainted by it no matter what. You may have no choice but to resign."

"So, it's hopeless?"

"Well, when my clients have hopeless cases I sometimes recommend them to a fixer I know. His measures may be a bit radical. I can call him, have him give you a call."

"Yes, do that, please."

"I'll call as soon as I get off the phone with you. But Jonathon…"

"Yes."

"I have no connection to whatever it is he does for you, is that understood? No connection and no knowledge."

Parsons gave his assent and hung up. His lawyer would call the "Fixer" and he would call Parsons back.

A half hour or so later the phone rang and a raspy voice asked for Jonathon Parsons.

"This is me," answered Parsons.

The raspy voice told him he had been asked to call by Parson's lawyer but had not been told the details.

Parsons quickly went over the facts and waited for a comment.

"What you want is to remain CEO of your company but not have the details of the divorce affidavit leaked to the press?"

"Exactly."

"That affidavit is part of a court file. Anybody who knows it is there can get a copy and even get it certified by a court clerk. Your real problem is the guys who now know it's there. All they have to do is tip off a member of the press to its existence and you will be revealed to the world as an accused child molester. When that happens, you won't have much choice but to resign. You have to stop these guys from leaking that information and get them to stop their tender offer for your company's stock. I don't think there is much I can do for you. You're in a hole, my friend. If you are willing to take the low road, I might be able to refer you to someone who could help. It will be risky and very expensive."

"What do you mean 'the low road'?"

"I mean are you willing to do anything, and I mean anything, regardless of how unethical, to save yourself?"

"I am. What do I have to do?"

"Contact this person through e-mail. Their address is 'medusa199@Mail.RU' and tell them your story and identify the people who are creating this problem for you."

"What kind of e-mail address is that?"

"It's a Russian e-mail service. I don't know if this person is Russian or not but they probably route their e-mail connection through numerous servers all over the place to avoid detection. Don't take this route unless you are willing to break the law, and you will have to be willing to pay. This service is very expensive, but I'm told by people I trust they are reliable and very good at what they do."

Parsons sat down at his computer and carefully composed an e-mail to "medusa199" explaining his situation and asking if there was anything that could be done to help him. It was several hours later that he discovered a response on his cell phone.

Your situation can be remedied. My services will cost you two hundred and twenty thousand American dollars. One hundred thousand dollars is payable immediately with the balance to be due when your problem is solved. If this is acceptable, I will respond with an offshore bank account number to which you can transfer the initial payment.

Parsons sat in the dark in his home study for over an hour looking off into space before he typed out a response to "medusa199."

Your proposal is acceptable.

Twenty-one
San Pedro, California

I packed a little overnight bag to go to Ariella's place. I felt kind of silly, like a kid going away to camp with his belongings. I wondered if I should have put name labels in my underwear. I had no idea where I was going for the weekend. I obviously had no stuff like toiletries or a change of clothes there so I had no choice.

The grey Camry pulled up in front of my condo right on time. I saw it out the window, picked up my bag and tried to walk out as casually as I could.

Ariella popped the trunk for me to put in my bag. I got in next to her and she gave me a big kiss. She was dressed casually in a dark blue tank top and light blue jeans with a pair of black espadrilles on her feet. She looked just as beautiful dressed this way as she had when she was in a silk dress with stiletto heels.

We pulled out and she headed for the Palos Verdes Peninsula. We cruised to Palos Verdes Drive North and took it all the way to Western and turned right. Along here, Western is bordered almost entirely by strip malls, grocery stores, Trader Joe's, liquor stores, bakeries, chain restaurants, that sort of thing. We turned left on First Street off Western and careened down the hill toward the harbor, driving through neighborhoods of wooden, craftsman-style bungalows built in the nineteen-twenties and thirties. From the road, we could see the harbor below in the distance. These distinctly blue-collar neighborhoods did not seem like a place where a high roller like Ariella would live, but we continued driving towards San Pedro's downtown area.

San Pedro used to be a separate town from Los Angeles but it was annexed by L.A. in 1909, primarily because of its large, protected harbor. The area has always had a unique character, in part because of the presence of large enclaves of Greek, Italian and Serbian/Croatian immigrants, who for years dominated a thriving local fishing industry. In recent years, the fishing hasn't been so good and the large tuna canning plants on nearby Terminal Island which depended on San Pedro fishermen's catch have closed. Fewer boats go out now and their catch is smaller. For many years the downtown area was sleazy with bars and flophouses catering to the sailors who passed through.

In recent years the area has cleaned up some, but the town is still largely blue collar, the housing old and the atmosphere more redolent of 1950s San Francisco than anything in twenty-first century L.A. San Pedro has a hilly topography surrounding an oblong harbor protected by jetties and the outcropping of the Palos Verdes Peninsula. Although a lot of shipping has gone to nearby Long Beach Harbor, the Port of Los Angeles, as it is officially named, is plenty busy with container ships, even cruise ships docking offloading cargo and passengers.

Ariella continued to drive down First Street first past Gaffey with its collection of run-down shops and ethnic restaurants, then past Pacific Avenue with more of the same. She was playing a Miles Davis, Thelonius Monk tune through the radio from her phone. "Are you sure you live all the way down here?" I asked as we approached the harbor.

"We're almost there, Fred. I told you it would be hard to find if you came by yourself. You'll see why in a few minutes."

We were no longer in a residential neighborhood, but surrounded by old brick and cinder block warehouses. In the one hundred block of First Street, the last block before you crossed the harbor side drive into the harbor itself, she turned into a driveway with a canvas-lined mesh gate next to an old, windowless, white-painted, brick warehouse. She tapped a button on her dash and the gate opened up. She pulled around to a shallow ramp in the warehouse wall leading down to a solid garage door. She tapped another button and the door began to open.

"This is where you live?" I almost gasped.

"Don't be judgmental, Fred," she said with a laugh. "You may be surprised when you see it."

We pulled down into a large, dark, open garage. I noticed an older model Toyota Land Cruiser parked in the otherwise empty concrete floor space. She pulled the Camry up next to a stainless-steel elevator in the wall. We got out and walked to the elevator. Ariella put her right palm up against a glass panel next to the door, a light blinked and the elevator quietly opened. I noticed that there were four floors on the control panel inside the elevator. We were on "G." below that was a "B," and above that a "1" and "2." Ariella hit "1" and we quietly ascended.

When the door opened, we walked out into a huge, open room with white marble flooring. The room was surrounded by a balcony on all four sides supported by marble Doric columns and a large marble staircase leading up to the second floor of the balcony. The area we walked into had several modern couches and chairs upholstered in a burnt orange. The center of the room was occupied by a stereo in a large blonde wood case flanked by light blue horn speakers which I immediately recognized as Avantgarde Trios. Each unit consisted of three plastic or fiberglass molded horns, one each for bass, midrange and tweeter, suspended on metal frames. I subscribed to a couple of audiophile magazines and I knew these speakers were well over fifty thousand dollars a pair and the bass horns positioned in between them on top of the wood cabinet cost at least forty thousand dollars. On either side of the stereo setup were four marble steps leading up to a dining room setup with a large trestle dining table and a buffet placed just behind the stereo set in blonde wood matching the stereo cabinet. There were a number of doors off the main room on all sides and upstairs there were doors off the balcony which, I assumed, led to bedrooms.

"I'm impressed," I said quietly.

"I thought you would be," said Ariella with her usual smile. "There are just a couple of ground rules for guests. This room," she said pointing to a door next to the elevator, "is my office and it's off limits. So is the basement, the entire basement. You may have noticed the elevator has a floor under the garage. If I catch you in either place, I would probably have to kill you," she said, still smiling. "I'm going to put on some music to show off my system then grab a bottle of champagne. I'll be right back."

She walked across the room to a door on the other side and after a few minutes emerged with a stack of vinyl albums. She flicked on the tube amplifier and I saw over twenty tubes light up in the cabinet.

"Let's let it warm up. Can you help me get the champagne and glasses?"

I followed her past the stereo in the center of the room up the four steps into the dining area. Through a pair of double doors on the far end of the room we entered a large rectangular kitchen gleaming with stainless steel.

"I got the fixtures from a sale at a failed restaurant. To be honest, I don't cook much but I like the idea of having a fully functional kitchen. Who knows, maybe someday I'll find a nice man who will cook for me?" she said, glancing at me.

At the far end of the galley-style kitchen was a large double-door Traulsen refrigerator. She opened it and grabbed a bottle of Roederer Cristal. I noticed there were at least another six bottles in the refrigerator. On the way out, she directed me to grab some champagne flutes from the buffet along with a crystal wine bucket which we took back into the kitchen and filled with ice from a stainless-steel, hotel-style ice maker.

Once back in the sitting area, she put the Miles Davis/John Coltrane album "Kind of Blue" on her Thorens TD 907 turntable.

She easily cracked open the Roederer and once again I marveled at the size and strength of her hands. We sat and sipped champagne while Davis and Coltrane exchanged licks. The music, through her incredible system, was simply thrilling, as if Miles and his band were right there playing just for us. The champagne was wonderful and I was completely dazzled by her home. "How did you ever manage this place?" I asked.

"It was an abandoned warehouse I picked up for next to nothing. I paid cash to have all the work done without permits. Obviously residential uses are not permitted in this area; it's zoned light industrial. As far as anyone is concerned this is just an old warehouse owned by an offshore corporation. I'm as anonymous here as I could be anywhere in L.A."

"That's right, you've always been clear about how much you

value privacy."

"Don't you, Fred? Do you want people peering into how you live your life and conduct your business?"

"Well, I'm in a regulated profession. My license to practice law depends on my following certain ethical rules, so I guess the State Bar retains the right to butt into my affairs when they feel they need to."

"I'm not real big on rules, especially not ethical rules, Fred. And in a way, my business consists of breaking the rules so I'm happier if no one is looking over my shoulder. I like being under the radar."

"I don't get it. How can your business be breaking the rules?"

She laughed, refilled my glass, got up to flip the record and sat down next to me on the orange couch.

"I refuse to answer on the grounds that this evening is intended for fun and play. When I think you're ready to know more about my business, Fred, I'll tell you."

She leaned over and kissed me. Her tongue invaded my mouth and wrapped itself around mine drawing it into her mouth. She promptly bit it and pulled away as I yelped in pain and handed me my glass.

"Champagne is very effective at deadening the pain. I have plenty on hand. You'll need it because it's going to be a very painful night."

She smiled at me but there was something in those huge blue eyes, something both distant and predatory, that frightened me.

After killing the bottle of Roederer, she suggested we bring in dinner from a local Vietnamese restaurant and watch a movie. I liked this idea better, a little better anyway, than having my tongue bitten.

I noted to Ariella there did not seem to be a television anywhere and wondered where we would watch a movie. She told me not to worry.

We both took the elevator down to the garage and drove to a little Vietnamese place on Pacific Avenue. We got imperial rolls with crab, fried rice and a sliced chicken breast dish with chili sauce.

When we got back to Ariella's warehouse, we got plates and silverware from the kitchen and she had me grab another bottle of champagne from the refrigerator. I followed her with my plate and the champagne as she walked to the far wall on the other side from the elevator and opened a door which led into a home theater set up.

There was a large white screen on one end and a projector in the back and a series of lounge chairs arranged around the screen, each with a small side table. "How about *Lady From Shanghai*?" she asked. "Do you like Orson Welles?"

I easily answered yes and she disappeared through a small door in the back of the room to load the Blue Ray.

We settled in with the second bottle of Roederer and the food while watching Welles' character get manipulated by Rita Hayworth and her movie husband. After the food was gone, Ariella took my hand. Somewhere in the last third of the movie she put it on pause to get another bottle of champagne.

A couple of hours later, thoroughly drunk, we wandered up the stairs to the second level. Ariella's bedroom was huge with a massive walk-in closet full of expensive clothes and a bathroom with soaking tub and separate shower. Ariella undressed in front of me. Her seemingly perfect body sent shivers down my spine.

The slap immediately sobered me up. I wasn't surprised. I knew from last time how this was going to go and I found myself trembling with excitement.

Twenty-two
Hermosa Beach

Lindsay was lurking on the sidewalk across from Fred's condo when the gray Camry pulled up and Fred jumped in. The girl at the wheel was drop-dead gorgeous. It had to be the one from the bar in Chinatown Fred talked about. She had long black hair and even from across the street Lindsay could see she had smooth, pale skin. When she glanced out the side window to pull away from the curb, Lindsay got a good look at her face and there was something familiar about it. She was pretty sure it was from high school but there was something else about the girl, something weird.

When she went home, she pulled out her Leuzinger High School yearbooks. The ones from sophomore, junior and senior year revealed nothing. But when she got to her freshman yearbook, she found her. Her name was Ariella Blumkin and she was a senior when Lindsay was a freshman. The picture was clearly her: long black hair with a slight curl, huge blue eyes and distinct cheekbones. The face was a little plumper than the girl in the gray Camry and the hair now was cut more sophisticatedly, slightly layered instead of flipped. Even so, Lindsay was sure it was the same girl, but there was something else.

She went to her laptop and googled "Blumkin." Among the search results was an article about a mass killing of a family in Lawndale. The mother, her son and her elderly father-in-law had been found in their condo with their throats slit. The mother and her father-in-law were Russian Jewish immigrants. At the bottom of the article was a paragraph noting that the sole surviving family member, as the husband had died several years earlier in a car accident, was a daughter who had been studying at the El Camino Junior College library the night of the murders.

Lindsay remembered someone at school remarking that the girl whose family had been murdered had been a student at Leuzinger the year before. She wondered if Fred knew about the messy past of his new girlfriend.

Lindsay wondered if the murders had ever been solved. The article said no fingerprints or other evidence had been found at the condo. There was no evidence of a robbery. She could find no follow-up articles about an arrest in the case.

So, Fred was now dating the surviving member of a family who had been massacred. It surely must have screwed with her head. Unless, she thought, Ariella was the killer. She laughed out loud at the thought. Whoever massacred the Blumkin family was a monster. The pretty, well-dressed girl in the gray Camry might be a lot of things, but Lindsay doubted she was that kind of monster.

Twenty-three
New York City

It was a warm spring day on Wall Street. In his office at Talisman Management, Jesse Blake was reviewing spreadsheets showing the acquisition of stock in Apollo Health.

Another five thousand shares and Talisman would have effective control over the board of directors, at which point they could call a special meeting to replace existing management with their own people who would start implementing their policies.

The plan, as outlined by Paul Voca, was to strip Apollo of as much overhead as possible to maximize profits. This would mean laying off employees, cutting benefits, closing some facilities and shutting down some of the tech research being done. Once the year-end profit and loss statement was released, Voca anticipated a major spike in Apollo's stock prices and he would begin selling.

The office was quiet and Blake realized it was already past seven. He was in no hurry to get home to his wife and children to whom he had nothing to say, who had nothing of interest to say to him.

He decided, as he often did, to stop in at The Full Shilling bar over on Pearl Street. The bar was moderately crowded, full of traders and hedge-fund types bragging to each other about their day's conquests. He managed to find a table against the wall opposite the bar and ordered an Irish whiskey on the rocks. A broker he knew passed by him, they greeted each other and he sat down for a few minutes to chat. Blake ended up buying him a drink and the two discussed the plans for a public offering by a small tech firm Paul Voca had taken an interest in. The broker tried to sound him out to see if Blake knew Voca's plans to acquire stock in the public offering. The reality was that Blake was Voca's hatchet man, used to pressure company executives and rile up shareholders in anticipation of takeovers. Blake was not privy to Voca's long-range plans. The guy was a genius but he trusted no one and Blake was content to play his role in the organization.

They talked for longer than he realized. When the broker got up to go back to his party, Blake realized it was past eleven. He should call his wife but she was probably already asleep, and besides, she was used to his late nights. He paid his tab and went out onto Pearl Street to hail a cab but the street was entirely empty and there were none in sight. A woman approached him. She was tall and blonde with a pair of dark-rimmed glasses. She was wearing a raincoat even though the night was clear and it had not rained for days. As she got closer, he could see she had a pretty face with nice defined cheekbones and beautiful blue eyes. She smiled at him as she approached.

"I am so sorry but the battery on my cellphone ran down and I really need to call my girlfriend to tell her where I am. Could I borrow yours? Just for a short call? I'd be so grateful."

Her smile was disarming and to Blake she looked like a disoriented out-of-town tourist so he nodded his assent and pulled out his cellphone to hand her.

She stepped toward him, her right hand out to take the phone. "Thank you so much and they say New Yorkers are not friendly," she said.

To his surprise, as he saw her hand, he noticed she was wearing latex gloves. He had no idea that her left hand plunged a knife into his chest until he saw the blood spurting all over his shirt. His knees buckled and he toppled over. The woman neatly sidestepped him as he collapsed, stooped to remove his wallet from his back pocket and turned into a nearby alley.

A cap to a sewer line in the alley was already partially opened. She moved it aside and deposited a blonde wig, glasses, switchblade, raincoat, latex gloves and Blake's wallet and phone. She could hear the sewer water running below as she carefully replaced the cap.

A now dark-haired woman without glasses in jeans and a long-sleeved cotton blouse continued walking in the alley away from Pearl Street, whistling in a high, clear tone the Thelonius Monk standard "In Walked Bud." In the background, back on Pearl Street, the sirens had already started.

Twenty-four
San Pedro, California

The weekend with Ariella went very well. On Sunday morning she asked me to cook breakfast for her. I was a little surprised but I didn't mind. I'm handy in the kitchen and she had everything we needed, eggs, bacon, bread for toast.

Her kitchen was a delight to cook in, well equipped with top-notch appliances and the best utensils. Afterward we took a long walk around the harbor and surrounding neighborhoods. We had an early dinner at a little Mexican place at First and Pacific then walked all the way back to her warehouse pad. She didn't talk a lot but she was affectionate the whole day.

After dinner we opened up some champagne and listened to music for hours, Monk, Miles Davis, Chet Baker, Art Pepper, even some old Louis Armstrong and Nat King Cole piano combos. Ariella would comment about the music. She was a veritable encyclopedia of jazz history. "Do you get lonely living here all by yourself?" I asked between albums.

"Not really, I'm pretty self-sufficient, but it's been nice having you around this weekend. You're easy company," she said, smiling. "I spend a lot of time traveling so when I'm home it's just a time to relax. I get plenty of excitement from my job. By the way, I'm going to be out of town for the next couple of weeks but maybe when I get back, we can do this again?"

Of course, that was all right with me. My idea of a good time definitely included sitting around drinking French champagne listening to great music on a world-class stereo system then having kinky sex with a beautiful woman.

"I'm curious, you have this beautiful home, this incredible stereo system, you could obviously afford to drive any car you wanted, a Bentley, a Ferrari, a Lamborghini or a Maserati, at the very least a Mercedes or a Beamer. Why do you drive an older Camry?"

"I like flying under the radar. I don't like being noticed. What could be more inconspicuous than an older gray Camry? There are tens of thousands on the road in L.A."

"I guess I just don't get it. Why worry about being noticed a little bit because you drive a nice car? Hell, in L.A., a BMW or Mercedes isn't much more noticeable than a Toyota "

"Well, Fred, I do have a cautious side, which you may understand better as you get to know me."

With that she drew me to her and gave me a long, hard kiss. From our time together I could tell she had impeccable personal hygiene and she kept her place immaculately clean. She told me she was not comfortable bringing in a maid so she did all her cleaning herself.

She disappeared for another couple of weeks during which I did not hear a word from her. When she got back, she called me and we reprised a weekend at her place. The first night we brought food in from a local Croatian restaurant and watched a Fellini movie, *Juliet of the Spirits*. The next day something weird happened.

That Saturday she told me she needed to go to the salon to get her hair and nails done. She showed me to a large room at the far end of the main sitting room. It was a library lined with bookshelves filled with books. There was a long table and some chairs in the middle of the room and a large Corbusier chaise with a side table in the corner of the room. "Read whatever you like, Fred," she told me. "I'll only be a couple of hours, then we can maybe go to Point Fermin and take a walk along the cliffs."

Once she left, my curiosity got the better of me. First, I went to the door she had told me was her office and tried to open it. It was locked. I remembered the "B" on the elevator and wondered if there really was a basement. I walked over to the stainless-steel door to the elevator and noted there was no palm print locking device on this one. I pushed the button and the elevator silently rose and the door slid open. I stepped in and pressed the "B" button.

The elevator quietly descended and the door opened on a dark, narrow hallway. A series of doors lined the hallway. I went all the way to the far end of the hallway and opened the door to my left. It was a large wine cellar with rows of wooden racks. There must have been at least two hundred bottles of wine, each one tagged with a number around the bottle neck. There was a section for champagne that, by itself, must have had over fifty bottles. I was duly impressed and moved to the door across the hallway.

To my shock it contained a miniature science lab with test tubes, Bunsen burners, racks of chemicals and a collection of glass beakers and porcelain mortar and pestles. It was like a well-equipped high school or college chemistry lab. I had no idea why Ariella needed a place like this. I left the lab and moved down the hallway to the next door.

This was an even bigger shock. It was an armory. There were racks of guns of all kinds, handguns, rifles, what looked like submachine guns and lockers of ammunition. It looked like something you might find at a police station or maybe a military base, not something you would find in the home of a beautiful young woman.

"Fred, you broke the rules," said a voice behind me. "I felt guilty abandoning you so I came back and I find you violating my privacy against my express instructions to you."

"I'm sorry, I shouldn't have, I was just curious, I…I didn't expect to find anything like this," I said stammering, feeling I had just destroyed our relationship for good.

"I like guns, Fred. I like guns a lot. So, I have a collection. It's a hobby. There's nothing wrong with that is there, Fred?"

"No, no, of course not." As always, I didn't anticipate the slap coming. This time it was harder than usual, a lot harder. For a moment I understood what people mean when they say a blow had them "seeing stars." I staggered back a few feet.

"On your knees, Fred."

As I sank to my knees, I was beginning to feel aroused despite, or maybe because of, being genuinely afraid of what she might do to me. As I looked up to her face, I realized that she was aroused too and I had no idea how this was going to end.

Twenty-five
J. Edgar Hoover Building, Washington D.C.

Chandler Diaz had over thirty open and active murder cases in which he was involved. These days he spent much of his time at his desk in D.C. directing investigators in the field. Like many agents he preferred field work to desk work but he had to admit to himself that running his section was more efficient than simply assigning individual agents or pairs of agents to cases. It also gave him a perspective on cases that identified patterns or similarities in disparate crimes. That is what he was beginning to see with several of the cases assigned to his unit.

The first and most surprising link was between the Tsing murder in Singapore and the Beckworth murders in New York. The offshore account to which Tsing's wife wired money was not the account of a financially troubled relative but an account which could be traced back to a Panamanian corporation, Medusa, S.A.

The offshore account to which James Beckworth had paid his "gambling debt," although a different account, could also be traced back to Medusa, S.A. The agent for Medusa, S.A. was a law firm in Panama City who were also the trustees of a trust which owned and controlled Medusa. The contents and identities of beneficiaries of the trust were protected by Panamanian law.

Diaz guessed the beneficiary of the trust was likely to be yet another offshore corporation that might well lead to yet another trust. Since the murders of James Beckworth and his sister, as well as their mother, were clearly linked to Medusa, S.A., this meant that at least seven murders were connected to the same source.

The Osorio murder in Florida was clearly directed by Venezuelan authorities who did not want their secret bank accounts to be publicized while the country spiraled into economic chaos. It now appeared the fatal dose of poison could only have been administered in the elevator as Osorio went down to the lobby.

Diaz' team finally located the maid who had been assigned to the cart that had been in the elevator with Osorio. Her partner that day was a temporary worker she never saw before. The maid described her coworker of that day as having long dark hair and large blue eyes. Although her skin was very pale, she spoke perfect Spanish and told her that she was from Colombia. The maid did remember the woman accidently bumped into Osorio and apologized profusely in Spanish. She recollected the woman professed to speak no English. Since that day she never saw the other maid again.

Diaz remembered the Amendola murder in Honduras involved a witness reporting a dark-haired woman nearby the small hotel where Amendola was killed who may have been the last person to see her alive. It was a tenuous link, but was it possible the killer in each of these cases was a woman? Certainly, the woman who apparently posed as a maid in a Miami hotel could have navigated comfortably in Honduras if she spoke perfect Spanish. Could these murders have been committed by the same person? Female professional assassins were rare but not unknown. This one, if indeed that's who it was, was talented.

Diaz' instincts told him the Amendola murder, which was being fruitlessly investigated by Honduran authorities, had been set up by outsiders. That could have been Atrios Financial who were financing the project and would make a tidy profit off it. Atrios was an American-based hedge fund. Diaz thought it might be fruitful to review Atrios' financial transactions around the time of the murder to see if there were payments that might look like they could have gone to a professional killer.

Twenty-six
Downtown Los Angeles

I met Eugene at a little *taqueria* on Broadway nestled between a discount appliance store, with signage only in Spanish and a clothing store featuring *quinceanera* dresses in the window. I had some *cabeza* tacos along with rice and beans and Eugene went with *carne asada*.

"So, let's hear all about your dream girl. I haven't talked to you since before your first weekend with her. How's it going?"

"Well, except for one little slip up," I said "Really good."

"What's her place like?"

"It's a palace. An old warehouse buried in an industrial section of San Pedro, by the harbor, that's been renovated. It's got a home theater, a commercial-style kitchen, a library, a wine cellar, lots of marble, luxury finishes. You should see her stereo system. It had to have cost her over a hundred thousand. From the outside it's just an old warehouse."

"The little slip up?"

"That's where it gets kind of weird. She took off one day to get her hair and nails done. She told me to stay out of her office and the basement level. So, her office was all locked up but I could take the elevator to the basement."

"What was in the basement?"

"Well, I mentioned the wine cellar, right? There must have been a couple of hundred bottles and I'm no wine connoisseur but I think it was all pretty good stuff."

"So why the big secret?"

"Well, the next room I checked out was like a chemistry lab with beakers and test tubes and chemicals and stuff. I have no idea what it might be for but I guess I wasn't supposed to see it. The next room was even weirder. Eugene, it was a gun room."

"Gun room?"

"Yeah, dozens of guns, handguns, rifles, assault rifles. I mean I know nothing about guns but there must have been one of almost everything you could ever get and plenty of ammunition too. The bad news was she caught me down there."

"Ariella caught you in the gun room, where you weren't supposed to be?"

"Yeah, she seemed pretty upset at first but it all kind of morphed into some pretty steamy sex. It was like the whole confrontation got us both aroused."

"Aah, now let's get on to the kinky sex."

"Well, let's just say we seem really compatible in that department and it's really gone well."

"So, are you forgiven for your slip up?"

"I think so, she hasn't mentioned it since then, I guess so."

"What do you think all that weird shit down in the basement is all about?"

"She says she's a gun collector, that she's really passionate about guns and she shoots at a local range every week, so maybe that's all there is to it?"

"Why forbid you to see it? What about the chem lab, what's that for?"

"I'm not sure why she would not want me to see her gun collection, but the girl is crazy private. I still don't know her last name or have a phone number for her. Is it so crazy she might want to keep her gun enthusiasm secret? Maybe she's afraid I'll think she's an NRA supporter or something? As for the chem lab, I don't think she knows I saw it. She caught me in the gun room and maybe thinks I didn't get any further. Anyway, we haven't discussed the chem lab and I am certainly not bringing it up."

"So, really, what is this strange girl like? When do I get to meet her?"

"She's hard to describe. Most of the time she's pretty quiet. She likes to be in control. She seems incredibly bright and very confident, like nothing would phase her. Of course, she is obviously very rich and has extremely expensive taste. I don't know when you will be able to meet her. Half the time she's out of town and she controls when we see each other. I'd like you to meet her and I'd like to get your take on her. I'll try to arrange a dinner or something."

"Lucques would be just fine, man, that is if she's paying. When do you see her again?"

"I have no idea. I've now spent three weekends at her place and that's been really nice, but it's been a couple of weeks since I've heard from her. I have no idea when I'll see her again."

We finished our tacos and talked about some other things. I was actually doing some work for his employer. We chatted about that for a while and when his next trip to Haiti was happening. We agreed to have lunch the following week and took our leave.

When I walked back into the office there was a phone call for me. "It's your friend Ariella," said my secretary, who now recognized her voice.

"Hey, Fred, sorry I haven't been in touch much the last couple of weeks I'm really busy and I'm about to take off for the East Coast but I have a proposition for you. Why don't you meet me in Panama after I'm finished with my project back east? I can get you a plane ticket and have a driver meet you at the airport to take you to my place. We can lounge by the pool drinking mojitos in the jungle."

Twenty-seven
New York City

Paul Voca had been disturbed by the murder of his assistant, Jesse Blake. The police wrote it off as a simple mugging gone wrong. There were no witnesses and no evidence. Several people saw him in the nearby bar where he had a few drinks and chatted with an associate. By the time he left the bar, the street was empty.

The police speculated there was someone lurking in the nearby alley waiting for someone who looked prosperous to come out of the bar. They felt they would have a chance to track down the perpetrator once Blake's credit cards were sold and used.

For Voca, the loss of his right-hand man and enforcer put some of his short-term plans on hold. He would have to find someone else with the same ruthless disregard as Blake to pressure management in companies who were resisting Voca's takeovers.

Blake was willing to play dirty, as dirty as required. He would not be easy to replace. Voca did wonder whether or not Blake's tactics led to someone taking revenge. The police assured him everything about the crime, the weapon, the time of day, the missing wallet, the seeming randomness of the encounter, pointed to a mugging. Perhaps Blake resisted or refused to give up his wallet or gotten verbally aggressive with his attacker.

For several years now Voca took his own security seriously. He had a bodyguard with him whenever he was away from his home. The Mercedes limousine he traveled in had bulletproof glass and light armor and the driver was armed. It was unlikely the Wall Street and corporate types with whom Voca competed would resort to physical violence. There were large sums of money involved, and, as Voca knew better than anyone, large sums of money tend to bring out the worst in people.

It was seven P.M. on a Friday night. Voca was supposed to meet some friends for a late-night dinner but he still had a little time. He went over to the bar in his office and poured himself a cognac. He could hear the cleaning people rattling around outside where his bodyguard was waiting for him.

Patrick Broussard, former NYPD officer and current bodyguard for Paul Voca, sat at a secretarial desk outside Voca's office waiting for the boss to finish up and head out to his dinner at Augustine around the corner. In many ways this was the best job Broussard ever had. The hours were long but his duties were simple and stress free. When Voca went to Augustine to meet with business associates Broussard would get a discreet table near the back and a chance to order off the menu. He wouldn't drink wine but he could count on having a fine meal, accompanying Voca home, then being dropped off at his own place by Voca's driver.

Broussard was a twice-decorated member of the NYPD and he was handy with a Glock. He had a concealed carry permit and always carried. The reality was Voca had never been in any actual danger. He had received a few threats over the years but no one had ever lifted a finger against him so Broussard's role was largely symbolic.

A janitor was flitting around the desks in the area while Broussard flipped through a copy of *Cosmopolitan* he found in a desk drawer. He noticed there was only one janitor, a shapely redhead. There was usually a crew of three or four that moved through the office. "Hey, where's the rest of your crew? You workin' alone tonight?" he yelled at the woman.

She turned around and smiled at him.

"The rest of the crew is on the eleventh floor but they sent me on ahead to get started up here to speed things up a little, you know."

Broussard thought she was pretty cute, with thick dark-rimmed glasses and red hair. Her gray cotton janitorial uniform did not disguise a lush, curvy figure. He smiled back and went back to his *Cosmopolitan*. He was laughing at an article that advised women how to achieve a satisfying orgasm when he felt cold metal at the back of his head.

"I'm so sorry to have to do this," she said calmly as she pulled the trigger of the nine-millimeter Beretta she held to his head. The silencer affixed to the muzzle emitted a faint pop and Broussard toppled out of his chair oozing blood from a hole in his forehead all over the *Cosmopolitan* which had fallen from his hands.

In his locked office, Paul Voca had not noticed any commotion outside as he began to pack his briefcase for the evening. Suddenly, the lock was blown off the double doors to his office and a young red-haired woman dressed in a janitor's outfit stepped through the door holding a pistol in her outstretched arm. She squeezed off a single shot that hit Voca square in the forehead. The redhead walked back to her janitorial cart and headed to the freight elevator at the back of the building.

Once down in the basement she pulled out a small overnight bag from the janitorial cart and took a pair of jeans, a blouse, and converse sneakers out, along with a light jacket. She changed out of the gray janitorial dress, pulled off the red-haired wig, stuffed that, the dress, the glasses, and her latex gloves into the bag along with the Beretta and a spare clip she was carrying. She slipped out the delivery entrance into an alley behind the office building with the bag slung over her shoulder.

When she emerged out onto the street, she walked three blocks and hailed a cab. "Take me to East River Drive," she told the cabbie. "I'll tell you where I want to get out."

When they got to the banks of the East River, the cab slowed and she got out, paying the cabbie in cash. She found a couple of bricks, some stones, loaded them into the overnight bag, then hurled it into the river. She walked another four blocks before finding a street with cabs. "Take me to JFK," she told the driver.

He dropped her off at the international terminal and she headed to the COPA Airline counter where she pulled an airline ticket out of her jacket pocket along with a Panamanian passport in the name of Maria Guisado. She got her boarding pass and headed through security to catch the one fifty-five A.M. flight to Panama City, Panama.

Twenty-eight
Buena Vista, Panama

I had never been out of the country except for a brief family vacation to Canada when I was twelve. It was exciting and maybe a little scary to be flying down to Central America by myself. I was booked out of LAX on COPA Airline to Panama City. From there Ariella promised to have a driver pick me up and take me to her house which was a couple of hours southeast of the airport.

To my surprise Ariella booked me in first class. As far as I could see, the big difference between first class and coach on COPA, besides being in the front of the plane, was more leg room and free alcoholic beverages. I ordered a rum and coke, and settled back in my seat for the six-hour flight.

Somewhere along the way I fell asleep. I was awakened by the captain's announcement we would be landing in a half hour. Below me I could see the skyline of Panama City, a crest of skyscrapers on the horizon. Panama City was obviously a major metropolis but the main airport, Tocumen, is about twelve-and-a-half miles south of the city. We passed to the west of the city over blue water, gradually descending. Tocumen was surrounded by green fields and a scattering of industrial buildings. When we landed, I grabbed my carry-on from the overhead bin and stepped out onto the jet way. I was immediately overcome with the heat and humidity. I followed the crowd to where a line formed for immigration. When I got to the immigration officer, she smiled, took my passport and looked me over, then snapped a picture of me with a stationary camera at her position and asked me to place my fingers on a glass pad that took my fingerprints. She stamped my passport and told me, "*Bienvenido*."

I had to put my carry-on bag through an X-ray machine and hand over my customs declaration to the customs official, after which I officially entered Panama. I made my way through the terminal toward the main entrance. Guys in green shirts crowded me asking if I needed a taxi. Ariella told me she would have me picked up so I supposed I didn't need a taxi, and besides, I would have no idea where to tell it to take me so I continued out the doors of the terminal.

The heat and humidity hit me even harder out there even though a strong breeze was blowing. There were lines of white taxis lined up on the curb. Off to my left I noticed a little gray-haired man with a handwritten sign that said "Cornwall," and figured that must be my ride. He had unkempt gray hair and a thick gray mustache. He was dressed in an old *Space Jam* T-shirt and baggy khaki pants.

"*Señor Cornwall?*" he asked.

I nodded and he directed me to an old white Toyota Corolla parked at the curb behind the line of taxis. He loaded my bag into the trunk and insisted I sit in the back.

We exited the airport and took a narrow paved road past warehouses, gas stations and other industrial buildings of indeterminate function. Off to my left I could see the skyline of Panama City but we were headed away from the city in a direction I guessed was east. After a few miles the buildings were left behind and we began seeing large pastures with humpbacked brahma cattle nestled between stands of thick, green forest. After almost ten miles, we merged with a wider four-lane highway and I got a glimpse of the canal to my left. The highway ran parallel to the waterway and I could see huge ships waiting for the locks to open. We drove this way at about fifty miles an hour for at least twenty miles before we pulled off onto another two-lane highway toward a line of green hills in the foreground.

As we headed south on the narrow road, the farms and pastures were fewer. The forested areas seemed to close in on the road, the trees tall and the underbrush dense.

After a while there were no more farms and we were just driving through thick jungle. At one point, a furry little animal with a pointed snout and a long tail held upright scurried across our path. "*Coati*," said the driver, the first words he had uttered since we left the airport. I wasn't sure if he was identifying the animal we almost hit or making a comment, so I just grunted in response. After a while we began to climb in elevation and crossed a few streams over one-lane bridges. We saw a couple of small waterfalls but no more pointy-snouted creatures. Finally, in the middle of nowhere, we turned onto a dirt road that began to climb a heavily forested hill winding through dense jungle. Quite suddenly, we crested the hill, passed a decrepit old iron gate that leaned open and rolled into a semicircular driveway in front of a large, two-story beige stucco house.

The place was reminiscent of the mission style one sees so often in California. The large front door and all the windows were arched. The roof was an orange, brick-colored tile. The driver, whose name I never did find out, retrieved my bag from the trunk and walked me through the arched double doors. I walked into a foyer, to the left of which was a large flight of mahogany stairs leading to the second level presumably. To my right was a large, open living room with teak-framed upholstered furniture. Directly in front of me was an extensive lounge area lined with arched French doors leading out to a large pool with a substantial tiled patio. In a chaise lounge by the pool I could just make out the lithe and shapely form of Ariella in a black string bikini reading a book. The floors were white ceramic tile and the light beige walls were covered with brightly colored primitive art featuring market scenes, jungle scenes and dark-skinned women with bandanas on their heads carrying baskets. Ariella put down her book and came into the house.

"Hey Fred!" she exclaimed sounding genuinely glad to see me, something which never ceased to surprise me. "Get your suit on and join me in a mojito. That's what I promised you, right?"

I tipped the driver, grabbed my bag and followed Ariella up the mahogany stairs. She showed me to a large corner bedroom overlooking the pool. I changed into bathing trunks and went back down to the patio where Ariella had the promised pitcher of mojitos.

"You have no idea how hard it is to find mint here." She laughed as she poured my drink.

I sat down next to her and reflected once again what a beautiful body she had, long legs, round hips, firm breasts, pale skin, all showcased by the brief bikini. I noticed the book she had been reading: *Intercourse* by Andrea Dworkin.

"That's a pretty lurid title," I said, referring to the book. "Is it pornography?"

"No, Fred. Far from it. In fact, it's a first-wave feminist tract. Pretty condemning of your sex, Fred."

"Wow, is that the way you feel about men?"

"I have to say I agree with a lot of it. Sexism and misogyny pervade every aspect of our culture, not the least of which is sex itself which so typically involves male domination. As you well know, Fred, I have my own solution for that problem. Let me show you around the house."

Both the lounge and living room were open to the foyer. The lounge had a large mahogany wet bar. The house formed a kind of "U" around the pool. The downstairs had two wings, one on either side of the lounge and living room. One wing contained an office, library and bathroom, the other a kitchen and dining room. Ariella pointedly noted that the office was unlocked and there were no "rules" in this house.

"I bought this place with furniture and décor included. The previous owner was some sort of mid-level drug lord who was killed decades ago. The estate had a hard time selling it because it's so remote. You can tell his taste in furniture ran to mid-century modern teak, which I have to say does not go badly with the style of the house. The paintings are mostly from Haiti, although there are a couple from Colombia. The house sits on a hill overlooking forty acres of land that came with it. As you can imagine it's very quiet, especially at night."

We walked back out to the pool where Ariella began to remove her bikini. "Since there's no one around and I'm not expecting anyone, there's no need for clothes. C'mon, Fred, shed those trunks."

I did and we both jumped into the pool, which was incredibly refreshing after the heat and humidity on the patio.

When we got out of the pool, she grabbed me and kissed me. As we kissed, she grabbed my testicles and began squeezing.

"Ow, that hurts," I exclaimed.

"I know," she said. "That's why I'm doing it." She pulled me by my testicles up the stairs to the bedroom.

We spent a couple of hours in the bedroom. At some point Ariella suggested we drive into the nearby town for dinner.

We climbed into an old Hyundai Tucson that was parked on the side of the semi-circular driveway and drove down the dirt road. Once on the paved road, we must have driven almost ten miles through dense forest before we came to a small town of low cinderblock buildings painted in pastel colors of green, pink and blue.

She pulled in front of a thatched-roof open-air pavilion with some chairs and tables. We were greeted in Spanish by the proprietor, a stout middle-aged woman, who seemed to know Ariella. We sat down and Ariella rattled off a long discourse in Spanish, the woman nodded and hustled off toward the tiny kitchen behind a counter in the back of the pavilion. "

There is no menu," said Ariella, "so I took the liberty of ordering for both of us. My impression is you're an adventurous eater so I ordered *lengua* for both of us."

I had been in enough Los Angeles *taquerias* to know that *lengua* was beef tongue, which, if prepared properly, could be quite good. Ariella was right: I would eat practically anything and I'm always curious about new foods. The waitress came back with two Panama beers in dark bottles. It was crisp, light and dry.

"I had no idea you were fluent in Spanish," I said.

"Fred, there are a lot of things you don't know about me," she said, flashing her huge blue eyes at me, "but I will help you learn and this trip should be a major lesson in the art of Ariella."

I was fine with that prospect. I had been impressed when she made a point that the office in the house was unlocked. I wondered if she expected me to wander in and go through the items on her desk.

"I seem to drink a lot when I'm with you. You never seem to feel the effects. We've gone through two bottles of champagne that left me blitzed and you seemed totally unfazed. I know you drink a lot, but have you ever been drunk?"

"Oh, I do feel the effects. I get more relaxed and comfortable. I'm a very controlled person, I rarely lose control. I never drink when I'm working. I guess I'm afraid I'd lose a step or two. That would be very, very bad."

"Have you ever done drugs?"

"No Fred, alcohol only. I never do drugs, just too much of a control freak."

Although it was six o'clock and the sun had just gone down, it was still warm, but a slight breeze blew through the little open-air restaurant as we sipped our Panamas.

The waitress came with two plates of meat in a tomato sauce, rice and black beans mixed together and a cabbage salad. To my surprise, the *lengua* was both tender and tasty. I was tired from the long flight and the strenuous, painful love-making that afternoon. The beer, food and the company of this strange, beautiful woman put me at ease.

That night, as we lay in her big, mahogany-framed bed, I began to hear thunder which became louder and louder. Flashes of bright lightning showed through the bedroom curtains, illuminating Ariella's naked body in the bed next to me. I could only reflect that she was a work of art, so incredibly lovely she seemed positively unreal, then the rain began. As a Southern Californian, my experience of rain is limited. Occasionally in our winter rainy season, a strong storm comes through. This rain was manic. It pounded on the roof above us so loudly I became afraid the roof would burst. There was something both terrifying and comforting in the intensity of this tropical rainfall. I found myself loving it.

As we lay there under the pounding rain Ariella's eyes snapped open. She looked directly at me and smiled. She crept over and climbed on top of me. Her hand went to my throat. Her grip was amazing. I began to struggle to breathe. She looked right down at me and smiled. I tried to tell her to stop but I couldn't speak. As she increased her grip on my throat, I passed out

In the morning I awakened alone in the bed. There were bruises on my neck that still hurt. I slipped on a pair of trunks and went downstairs. Ariella was out by the pool on her chaise with her book. She had a large white mug of coffee and a sweating tumbler of something that looked like pineapple juice.

"Hey Fred," she said, smiling, not putting down her book. "There is fresh coffee and cold pineapple juice in the kitchen. Help yourself. The coffee is local. It's from a place in the northern mountains called Boquete. You'll like it. When you wake up, there are eggs and bacon in the kitchen and I'll expect you to make me breakfast." This was something that had become a ritual with us. I didn't mind. After all, she seemed to pay for everything; the least I could do was cook breakfast.

After a cup of coffee, I found eggs, bacon, some white cheese and a Costa Rican *Chilera* salsa in the kitchen and threw together scrambled eggs and bacon. We ate on the patio by the pool.

"Today I thought we could take it easy and just relax by the pool. Feel free to grab a book from the library. Tomorrow we should head into Panama City. I need to see my lawyers there. We can stock up on provisions, maybe go to a club in the evening or seek some other type of recreation. Later today, I want to take a walk and show you something very special."

The library did not have the impressive collection of books she had in her San Pedro digs. I was able to find an old Michael Connolly mystery. I cleaned up the breakfast dishes and settled down by the pool.

We read for a couple of hours before Ariella told me she wanted to walk. She slipped on a cover-up and some flip-flops and we started down the hill on the other side of the pool. The house is on a hill surrounded by forest with the pool patio overlooking a thick stand of jungle to which we were directly headed.

"We're not actually going into the jungle, are we?" I asked.

I was only wearing swimming trunks, a T-shirt and flip-flops and did not feel equipped to go on a jungle expedition. As we walked down the hill, several iguanas fled in front of us.

At the bottom of the hill Ariella headed right into the line of trees. I followed her into a dense, dark, humid world that made me feel a bit frightened and claustrophobic. She forged fearlessly ahead as I began to wonder if we could find our way back. As we walked, the trees grew taller and a heavy, musky smell pervaded the forest. The undergrowth was dense but she appeared to know her way. I followed faithfully behind.

After seemingly walking through the heavy brush forever, I saw a shaft of light ahead in what seemed to be a small clearing. Ariella led me to an old thick-trunked tree covered with moss. About eight feet off the ground was a beautiful flower with split black petals and a flash of orange at its center. The flower was growing off the tree but not a part of the tree.

"It's a black orchid," said Ariella.

"It's beautiful," I said sincerely.

In the middle of the dark forest, in a sea of green, here was this delicate and lovely flower showcased by the sunlight entering the tiny clearing. "It's perfect."

"Experts will tell you there is no such thing as a black orchid, just dark blue ones. Here we are and here it is. Wouldn't you say this is black, Fred?"

"No doubt. It's beautiful and sinister, just like you." I realized as I said this that I may have just insulted her and I prepared to take back my words.

Instead she seemed pleased. Her usually bland, ambiguous smile lit up into something like a genuine one.

"Exactly like me, Fred."

We spent the rest of the day relaxing and drinking bottle after bottle of champagne. She apologized that it was just Moët and Chandon White Star and not the premium Roederer we drank at home.

"It's all I can get here," she said.

As evening drew near, she suggested we go back to the little restaurant in town. "After all the champagne can you drive?" I asked.

I was quite drunk myself.

"No problem, Fred, I never drink to excess," she answered even though she probably out-consumed me two to one and we had gone through four bottles of White Star. True to her word, Ariella drove flawlessly into the little town and ordered us both Panama beers and *arroz con pollo*.

The food sobered me up a bit and Ariella drove us both back to the house where we ended up going to bed early, tired from soaking up so much sun and champagne. We had been asleep for a couple of hours when the thunder, lightning and rain woke me up.

Once again, the rain came crashing down on the roof above us. Ariella did not wake up. I watched her in her sleep, breathing shallowly and reflected on what a strange woman I had gotten mixed up with. I never quite knew what was going on in her mind and most of her life was still a mystery to me.

The next morning, she got me up early. We had a quick breakfast then took off in the Tucson for Panama City. It was still drizzling when we left, the sky slate gray and threatening. We each took an overnight bag since Ariella told me we would stay the night, get a hotel room and return in the morning. She wanted to explore some clubs at night, not wanting to make the drive when it was pitch black and we were tired and drunk.

For most of the way, the drive there was just a reversal of my ride from the airport. However, we did not get off the main highway until we got into town. Ariella maneuvered the Tucson through the streets of the outlying city into the district called *Casco Viejo*, the old town. She booked a suite at the Central Hotel Panama in the heart of the old district. When she registered, I was surprised to see her take out a Panamanian passport. She noticed my surprise and as we walked to the room said, "In Panama, for most purposes, my name is Maria Guisado, so please don't act surprised."

"Are you hiding something?" I asked.

"I'm hiding lots of things, so you might as well get used to it," she replied.

The suite on the top floor was lovely. Despite the Victorian look of the hotel it was modern with hardwood floors and streamlined furniture. The bathroom was fully tiled floor to ceiling and two thick, white, terrycloth robes hung next to the shower.

"We need to get to my lawyers' offices in the new city within the hour, so let's stow our bags and grab a taxi," she told me.

Her lawyers' office was in a skyscraper in the new section of town that contained a cluster of tall buildings looking out over the Pacific Ocean. The conversation was entirely in Spanish but I did note that she was greeted as *Señorita Guisado*. I could not follow most of the rest of the conversation but I thought I made out something like "FBI" and *"Isla*

Cayman." Ariella seemed calm throughout the discussions so I assumed there was nothing for her to be worried about. The "FBI" reference could have been about some bank or something. We were there for about an hour and a half and while they offered us some excellent coffee, we were famished by the time we left.

Ariella, or should I say "Maria," seemed to know her way around and we walked to an elegant seafood restaurant on the ground floor of one of the tall buildings. We ordered grilled fish and a bottle of Chilean sauvignon blanc.

"Is everything okay?" I asked.

"My money is still where it's supposed to be," she said, "my investments are doing well. Everything's okay."

"Did I hear mention of the FBI?"

"You might have," she said smiling her ambiguous smile. "If there was, I'm not troubled by it."

"What reason might the FBI have for being interested in you?"

She looked at me appraisingly when I asked.

"I can think of a few things," she said, sipping her wine.

After lunch we went back to the hotel and relaxed for a couple of hours. We spent some time walking around the *Casco Viejo*. My impression of Panama City was always based on the photographs of clusters of skyscrapers like the one Ariella's lawyers' offices were in.

Panama City is very old. It was founded by the Spanish in 1519. In 1617 it was raided by the English privateer Henry Morgan and the resulting fire destroyed much of the original city.

Some of the ruins of that city still exist. The city was rebuilt on the present site of *Casco Viejo* which is now the historical core of the present bustling metropolis that has well over a million people in its metropolitan area. The *Casco Viejo* has narrow cobblestone streets and a collection of old buildings, some going back to the seventeenth century.

We spent time walking the streets. Ariella seemed to know the quarter well, would point out buildings and tell me their history. We stopped for dinner at a little Cuban café called *Habana Vieja* where we drank mojitos made with Cuban rum and ate garlic roasted chicken with rice, black beans and fried plantains.

Later that night we walked from the hotel to a jazz club in the *Casco Viejo* called Danilo's. We ordered more mojitos and listened to a small combo, saxophone, trumpet, piano, bass and *conguero*. They played hard driving Latin versions of old jazz standards like "Round Midnight," "Perdida," and "Just Friends." Judging by the smile on her face, Ariella was truly enjoying herself.

We went through several rounds of mojitos in a little over two hours. It was about eleven P.M. when Ariella said, "Okay Fred, it's playtime."

I assumed she meant it was time for us to go back to the hotel for her to choke or slap me some more. Instead we walked outside the club and she hailed a cab. She gave the driver an address in Spanish that meant nothing to me and we took off through the *Casco Viejo* to a part of town that looked old and foreboding. The streets were narrow and the tall, narrow, run-down buildings on either side of the street looked late nineteenth century. The taxi pulled up in front of a three-story building with crumbling stucco exposing the underlying brick. There was a heavy smell of salt in the air and I assumed we must be close to the harbor. A thick wooden door at the top of a short flight of stairs from the sidewalk was partially illuminated by a lamp with a red-light bulb.

She paid the cab and we climbed the stairs to the door. The entire neighborhood had an unpleasant musty smell to it. Ariella knocked and the door was answered by a slender middle-aged blonde woman in a black lace mantilla over a plain black dress.

"*Señorita Guisado*" she exclaimed apparently happy to see us.

She led us into a large sitting room with a bar on the side. The room was narrow with high ceilings and tall narrow windows obscured by thick scarlet curtains. There was a couch and several large easy chairs upholstered in red velvet to match the curtains surrounding a carved wood table. The floor was tile covered by a thick, rose-colored, Oriental wool rug. A doorway leading into the rest of the house was obscured with a curtain.

"*Señora* Leon, this is my friend, Fred. He speaks only English. We are both interested in indulging in your services here," said Ariella in English.

I wondered what services she could be talking about but I was beginning to get a feeling this was not the evening I expected.

"Of course, *Señorita*. May I assume that it is Mirabella whose company you seek to enjoy again? May I get you a drink while we wait for her?" asked *Señora* Leon.

"The answer to both questions is 'yes,'" answered Ariella.

Señora Leon went to the bar and poured caramel colored liquid from a rectangular glass bottle into two snifters and handed them to Ariella and me.

"This is eighteen-year-old *Flor de Caña* rum, Fred. You'll be surprised at how smooth it is."

The quality of the rum was not my primary concern at this point. We seemed to be in a bordello and my supposed girlfriend had requested a prostitute.

I had no idea what was going on but I was feeling pretty confused. *Señora* Leon asked, "*Señorita*, does your friend desire companionship as well?"

"*Si, Señora, traele un joven, uno muy joven.*" *Señora* Leon smiled, nodded and disappeared through the curtained door.

"Ariella, what the hell is going on?" I asked.

"It's play time, Fred. Get into the spirit, let's have some fun."

Before I could respond a stunning, young, light-skinned black girl walked into the room through the curtained doorway. She had golden curls hanging in ringlets to her shoulders, huge green eyes and an amazing figure. She wore light-blue baby-doll lingerie, blue stiletto heels and, as far as I could tell, nothing else.

"*Hola Maria, como esta? Estoy feliz de verte,*" said the girl to Ariella who seemed to be known as "Maria" here. The two embraced while *Señora* Leon appeared with another girl. This one, also dressed only in a baby-doll nightie, looked to be about fifteen. She was stunning in her own way. She had light copper skin, straight blonde hair, high cheek bones and thick cherubic lips under large brown eyes. Her breasts were small but distinct, supple. While she was perhaps only five foot four or shorter, she had a lush, shapely figure.

"Here you go, Fred, let her take you back and play," said Ariella with a smirk.

The girl took me by the arm and led me back through the curtained doorway to a flight of narrow stairs. Ariella and Mirabella followed us arm in arm. When we got to the second floor they disappeared into a door off the long hallway. We continued down to the end of the hall and through a door at the end. It was a small bedroom with a double bed on a brass bedframe. There was a small wooden wardrobe in one corner and I noticed a large wooden crucifix on the wall next to the bed with a porcelain Christ figure that had garishly painted red wounds. I thought to myself that this is wrong and resolved that I would simply wait out my time with this child-woman without doing anything I would go to jail for back home.

Unfortunately, I could not keep my resolution. The girl, whose name was Florinda, proved to be too aggressive and too skilled for me to resist. Our encounter lasted about forty-five minutes after which Florinda diplomatically gestured to me that my time was up and led me back to the front room downstairs. Ariella was nowhere to be seen. However, *Señora* Leon assured me that she would be down soon and poured me another snifter of rum. I had to admit to that it was very smooth.

I felt guilty about what I had done with the little teenager and thoroughly confused about what Ariella was doing with the beautiful black girl a floor above. When she finally came down about a half hour later, she embraced Mirabella and kissed her hard on the lips then went to *Señora* Leon and handed her a large wad of cash. She exchanged a few words in Spanish with her and turned to me. "Did you enjoy yourself, Fred?"

I felt myself blushing and could not muster a response. *Señora* Leon called us a cab and we drove back to the hotel. On the drive back Ariella turned to me with a smirk. "*Señora* Leon tells me that Florinda is only thirteen. She's quite well developed for her age. Wouldn't you say, Fred? *Señora* Leon says she is one of their most popular girls."

"I didn't do anything with her," I lied, suddenly feeling angry in addition to the confusion and embarrassment I'd been feeling.

"I don't believe you, Fred," Ariella said calmly. "I know you well enough to know you couldn't restrain yourself with that little tidbit.

What's wrong Fred, are you jealous of me being with Mirabella? After all I set you up with Florinda to balance the ledger."

"I just don't understand what kind of relationship we have. Yes, I am jealous that you were fucking someone else. I admit it."

"Did you think we were going steady, Fred?" Once again there was that smirk.

"I guess I just don't know what we are doing."

"I thought this was pretty casual, Fred, just play time. Do you want it to be more than just play time?"

"Yeah, that's what I've always wanted."

"Are you in love with me, Fred?"

She still had that smirk on her face, but I told the truth.

"Yeah, I think so."

"Fred, you've said yourself how little you know about me. Are you just beginning to learn?"

Just then the taxi stopped at the hotel. We got out and headed to the elevator. Once in the room Ariella called room service and asked for a bottle of champagne and some hors d'oeuvres.

"Are we celebrating something?" I said trying to be sarcastic.

"No, Mirabella gave me a real workout, Fred, so now I'm hungry. Didn't your child lover help you work up an appetite too?"

She began to undress removing her skirt and shoes. She was sitting on the bed in a pair of white thong panties, her bra and an open blouse. "Tell him to bring it in," she told me when I answered the knock at the door.

As the waiter wheeled the cart into the room, she slipped off her blouse and bra, walked over to her purse on the night stand to extract some money for the tip in only her panties. As she walked toward him the waiter's jaw dropped and his eyes grew wide. "*Muchas gracias,*" she said as she handed him the bills.

"*Con mucho gusto,*" he exclaimed as he scurried from the room looking both embarrassed and turned on.

The cart held a bottle of Mumms, two glasses, a tray of smoked salmon canapes, a small crystal dish of caviar and a tray of tiny toast pieces.

"Open the champagne, Fred," she said as she spread caviar on toast. She walked toward me and embraced me with a smoldering kiss. "I'm just all appetite tonight, Fred."

That night she was rougher with me than she had ever been.

The ride back to her house the next day was quiet. I had bruises in several places, including on the right side of my face. She was cool and quiet almost as if I were not there. We did stop at a tiny restaurant on the way for ceviche and beer but neither of us had much to say.

When we got back to the house Ariella shed her clothes and jumped into the pool. I had a headache and I was still sore and bruised from the previous night's activities. Mostly I found myself confused and upset over the state of our "relationship," whatever you wanted to call it. I was in no mood to frolic naked in the pool with her.

Instead I wandered into the house and found myself drawn to the office. There were papers scattered on the desk and an open laptop. To my shock the documents and the characters on the laptop were in some strange alphabet I had never seen before.

"It's Cyrillic, the Russian alphabet," said a voice behind me.

She was lounging in the doorway, knowing I could not look away from her naked body. "The language is Russian so even if you knew the alphabet you wouldn't understand any of it unless you spoke Russian."

"Are you a Russian spy?"

"Hardly. My parents left Russia because they were Jews who were being persecuted. They hated Russia and so do I. I grew up speaking and writing Russian at home. My grandfather never did learn English. What you are looking at are the notes from my last project. I'll destroy them before we go back to L.A."

"So that's why you said the office wasn't off limits. You knew I couldn't read a thing in here."

"I'm flattered you find me so interesting you spy on me, Fred."

"Look, I care about you and I want to know everything about you."

"Really, Fred?"

"Yes, absolutely."

"Let's take a walk Fred. Let's go see if the orchid is still there."

She threw on a cover-up and some flip flops and we went down the hill like before. As we approached the tree line, we saw a troop of large, brown, white-faced monkeys in the trees overhead. There were bright blue and yellow butterflies at the base of the trees feeding on the flowers there. As before, I trudged after Ariella completely disoriented and a little afraid of the impinging jungle.

The orchid was still there. "I liked what you said about me, Fred. That I was beautiful and sinister. I liked that a lot."

"You liked being called sinister?"

"Do you really want to be part of my life, Fred?"

"More than anything."

"What I'm about to tell you can't be repeated to anyone, is that clear, not anyone?" Her large blue eyes had a peculiar light as if she were being possessed by something.

"Okay, I can keep secrets," I said, thinking to myself how big a deal could anything she told me really be?

"I kill people, Fred. That's my work. I'm really good at it and people pay me a lot of money to do it. I take the hardest targets, the ones with security or sequestered in safe places that others can't get. I like it, Fred, more than anything."

I started to laugh but the look on her face made me realize she was serious. Either she was crazy, completely nuts, or she was telling the truth, maybe both.

"If you want to be part of my life, Fred, you have to be part of that, too."

Twenty-nine
New York City

Jonathon Parsons was frightened to think that the FBI was paying him a visit. After news came out about the deaths of Jesse Blake and Paul Voca, it dawned on him that he was guilty of a serious crime. He had deleted all references to "medusa199" on his computer. He wired the second payment to Medusa as originally agreed upon. The killings stopped the acquisition of Apollo's stock and it seemed safe now that no word of his ex-wife's accusations would be leaked to shareholders. Things were back to where they were before the phone call from Jesse Blake and for that Parsons was deeply grateful. Now the FBI was coming to call.

The agent who arrived at his office was a tall, light-skinned black man dressed in a baggy blue suit with a checkered blue and white shirt and blue tie. He had large, sad-looking green eyes, and the faint outline of a graying beard and mustache.

"Mr. Parsons, I'm Special Agent Chandler Diaz and this is Detective Becky Haden from the NYPD homicide division."

He was referring to a petite blonde woman with piecing blue eyes in a tan pants suit and dark-blue striped shirt. Diaz specifically requested Haden after he was brought in following the death of Paul Voca. She was smart, energetic and, like him, she was a kind of outsider, one of the few women detectives in homicide. He, as a dark skinned Cuban-American, was an outlier in the upper regions of the FBI, so they both approached things from slightly different angles than their colleagues.

"Mister Parsons, what was your relationship with Talisman

Management?" asked Diaz.

"Well, I know they have a tender offer out for stock in my company. I've had a few conversations with one of their executives, Jesse Blake, about the company and their interest in it."

"Did anyone from Talisman tell you that you would be replaced as CEO once they had a controlling interest in Apollo?"

"No, I don't recall anyone saying anything like that."

"You are aware, are you not, that Talisman has a history of replacing the entire management team of companies it has gotten control over?"

"I'm not really that familiar with Talisman or its business practices."

"Were you at all troubled by Talisman's attempt to gain control of Apollo?"

"Well, I still have a lot of shares in Apollo and they were offering a good price. I stood to make a lot of money off their tender offer. It was a good deal for me." Parsons could feel his palms sweating and he hoped he did not look as nervous as he felt.

"Would it be a good deal for you even if they removed you as CEO from a company you founded?"

"I don't know that they would have done that. After all, it was my expertise that helped grow this company and make it so successful. As the controlling owners, I would have thought they could use my expertise to continue making the company profitable."

"When you had discussions with Mister Blake did you talk about problems he saw with the overhead of Apollo?"

"Yes, he had some legitimate concerns about how high our overhead had become and I agreed with him. Later on, I did a memo to shareholders telling them how we planned to reduce our costs and hopefully give a boost to our stock price."

"So as far as you remember your relationship with Blake and Talisman was friendly and business-like? There was no conflict?" This was from the woman detective.

"Right. Well, I only had contact with Blake. I never met anyone else from Talisman. Yeah, it was open and affable. He made it clear that

Talisman was going to do a tender offer on Apollo. Frankly, I found it flattering they thought my company would be worth buying."

He wondered if they could tell how warm he felt and how moist his palms were. Did he sounded calm enough to be believable?

"Several weeks ago, you wired one hundred thousand dollars to a Cayman Island bank account. Just last week you wired another hundred and twenty thousand to that same account," said the male FBI agent.

Parson's heart began to beat rapidly. Of course, they would have known about that. There was an electronic trail.

"You're not here representing the IRS, are you?"

"We're here investigating two murders, Mister Parsons," said Diaz.

"Well, to be honest I was just trying to shift some funds off-shore, you know, anticipating some hefty capital gains from the sale of my Apollo stock to Talisman, that's all." Parsons swallowed hard after saying this and shifted uncomfortably in his chair.

"Mister Parsons, that's all we needed to know. Thank you for your time. By the way, isn't the tender offer from Talisman off the table now that Blake and Voca are dead?" asked Diaz.

"It appears that way now, yes," said Parsons, almost visibly sighing with relief.

Diaz and Haden both smiled, nodded their heads and left knowing that Parsons had lied to them about the money.

Thirty
Hermosa Beach

Fred seemed to have disappeared for a while. It had been weeks since Lindsay had seen him at volleyball or at the bar afterwards. The past week she went by his condo on Second Street several times and there was no sign of life. The less she saw him, the more panicked she found herself about losing him entirely.

She knew she could not compete with a woman like that Ariella Blumkin. That girl, though, was way out of Fred's league. As much as Lindsay liked Fred, she could not imagine what a woman like that, with money and looks, would see in an ordinary guy like Fred. It must be some kind of con game to ensnare poor Fred.

Lindsay decided to try to do some research on Ariella. She went online and did a Google search. She was able to come up with Ariella's graduation from Leuzinger High School, El Camino Junior College and UCLA where Ariella graduated *cum laude* with a degree in Russian literature. After that she could find nothing. She even signed up for one of those people locator services that require a fee but there was nothing. It was as if, after graduating from UCLA, she fell off the face of the earth.

Lindsay remembered a friend of her sister's had been a classmate of Ariella's when they were at Leuzinger. She called her sister and got Eileen's number. She still lived locally in Torrance, was married and had a two-year-old daughter.

"Hey, Eileen, this is Lindsay Carpenter, Janet's sister, remember me?" she said in her most cheerful voice when she got Eileen on the phone.

"Sure Lindsay, I remember Janet's little sister. What can I do for you?"

"Well, this is gonna sound kind of strange but a friend of mine has sorta gotten involved with Ariella Blumkin, remember her?"

"A little. I have no idea where she is now. Frankly I'm surprised she's still around."

"Oh yeah, she is. I actually saw her the other day. Look, you knew her in high school. What was she like?

"Gosh, you know she and I weren't really friends or anything. I mean I had some classes with her and stuff. She was quiet, didn't have a lot of friends, but she was real smart, like one of the smartest kids in the school. In a lot of ways, she was pretty intimidating. She was really pretty, you know, but she kinda scared most of the boys away. I haven't heard anything about her since El Camino. I guess she went on to UCLA but I don't know anyone who knew her there."

"Wasn't there something about her family?"

"Oh yeah, I almost forgot. Her family was murdered while she was at El Camino. It was really grisly. What was weird is I saw her around campus a few times after that, I was going there too at the same time, and she seemed exactly the same, cool, calm, quiet, unruffled, like nothing happened."

"What was the deal with her parents?"

"As I remember, her dad died before she was even born, in a car accident or something. Her parents were from Russia, immigrants fleeing persecution or something. They come here, everyone gets killed, except her of course."

"Did they ever figure out who did it?"

"I have no idea. I just remember running into her a few times at El Camino right after the murders and her not seeming to be very rattled. I was amazed she was even still in school. She was one cool number, that girl."

"Do you know anybody who has seen her recently or even in the last few years?"

"No, not since Junior College."

"Didn't she have a best friend, a boyfriend or anything?"

"No, she never had a lot of friends, definitely no best friend. In high school I heard her mom would not let her date and I didn't know anyone in junior college who dated her. Like I said she scared away the boys. She was pretty, maybe too pretty for a lot of them to think they had a chance. There was also something about her that was a little bit different that may have kept guys away. Anyway, Lindsay, what's with all the questions? Why do you care about this girl?"

"A friend of mine, a nice guy I play volleyball with, has gotten involved with her and I'm a little worried about him. I think he may be in over his head."

"Wow, so she's still around. I don't blame you for being concerned. If your friend is really a nice guy, I really don't think she's the girl for him. Oh, wait, I do remember one incident from our junior year, before you were there. This girl was giving Ariella a really hard time, probably jealous of the pretty girl but also targeting a kid who was a little different. Finally, Ariella had enough. She turned on the girl, beat the living daylights out of her. It all happened in the school hallway between periods, a crowd gathered around and watched Ariella just put this girl down. She was strong and really vicious. Ariella got suspended but only for a couple of weeks. I mean, she was an A-plus student so they cut her some slack. After that everybody left her alone."

"Thanks, Eileen. I'll try to warn him but there really isn't anything specific I can tell him, it's just a feeling I have about her."

"Yeah, that's sorta the way I always felt about her too. You'd be doing him a favor by warning him."

Lindsay said goodbye, hung up and wondered how she could ever warn Fred if she never saw him.

Thirty-one

J. Edgar Hoover Building, Washington D.C.

Chandler Diaz now knew Jonathon Parsons had hired a professional killer to take care of Jesse Blake and Paul Voca. He knew this because the Cayman Island bank account to which he twice wired money was linked to the same Panamanian corporation as the account to which Vi Li Tsing's wife and James Beckworth wired money. He lied about the purpose of the fund transfers. It was now clear that the Tsing, Beckworth, Blake and Voca murders, a total of nine victims, were linked to the same murderer, perhaps to an organization that handled murder for hire.

The bank accounts were all different numbered accounts with the same Cayman bank. The Treasury Department, which monitored offshore banking, reported to the FBI that the owner of these accounts was Medusa, S.A., a Panamanian corporation registered with Benedict, Alfaro, Sabredo, *Abogados* in Panama City, Panama. The owner of the corporation was the Medusa Trust. Under Panamanian law the beneficiaries and trustees of private trusts were entitled to complete privacy. Legally it was impossible to obtain information regarding such trusts.

Treasury, however, had a source inside the law firm who had access to their files. This source indicated the beneficiary of the Medusa Trust was a Panamanian citizen named Maria Guisado. Using all the resources available to the FBI Diaz could find no information at all on Maria Guisado. There were no bank accounts, property owned or rented by, employment records, criminal records, driver's licenses or any other documentation of the existence of such a person. There were immigration records showing a person named Maria Guisado, using a Panamanian passport, entering Panama on a number of occasions and several records of such an individual exiting the United States but there was no record of her ever leaving Panama. While the Medusa Trust itself undoubtedly had bank accounts in Panama, the trustee and beneficiary of the trust were confidential. It would be impossible to link the trust to specific bank accounts. Even if they had a name of an account holder, if there was no official connection to an American citizen, information regarding that account holder would be unavailable to United States authorities.

Diaz would notify United States' Immigration and TSA to flag the name "Maria Guisado" on a Panamanian passport. Any attempt by a person with a passport under this name to enter or leave the United States would result in her being taken into custody handed over to the FBI for questioning.

It was possible that the person using this name was only a broker for an organization contracting out professional assassins and not the killer herself. There was no evidence that the killer in any of the cases to which Medusa, S.A. was linked was a woman. In Diaz's experience, very few professional killers were female. It was true that in the Osorio and Amendola cases there was some evidence indicating the possibility of a female killer, and one who spoke fluent Spanish, there was no reason to link them to the Singapore and New York killings. It was more than likely in these killings the killer was a man and Maria Guisado was his boss, a paymaster, a go-between or simply a pseudonym.

Thirty-two
Downtown Los Angeles

Eugene and I met in a little Oaxacan restaurant on Seventh Street just east of Broadway. I ordered a turkey *mole* and Eugene had a *tlayuda*, a tortilla with black beans, cheese, guacamole and pork. I had a watermelon *agua fresca* and Eugene had one made from tamarind. I was happy to see him for the first time in several weeks but eager to avoid any discussion of my trip to Panama, which, of course, is the first thing he brought up.

"Fred, you have to tell me how it went with the mystery woman in her tropical paradise."

"To be honest I'm just not ready to talk about it, if that's okay?"

"Oooh, that bad huh? You struck out under the tropical moon? The great romance is over?"

"I don't know. I'm not sure where we stand. Some very odd things happened there and I'm not sure what to make of them."

"Tell me, I'm here to advise."

"I can't talk about some of it, she swore me to secrecy and she really meant it. One thing that happened is she took me to a whore house in Panama City."

"She what? You're kidding right? Did she expect you to do a hooker? Why would she do that?"

"Well, it was for her, oh, actually for both of us. She had a girl she liked there."

"You are blowing my mind. Your girl went with a hooker? She's bisexual?"

"Yeah, I guess, I don't know. But she got one for me too."

"Oh man! So you guys went whoring together? That is so wild. How was she, your hooker, was she any good?"

"Yeah, she was really good," I sighed, "and then Ariella tells me afterwards she's only thirteen." Eugene started giggling.

"My god, you're a child molester!" he said laughing.

"I wasn't going to do anything with her, I knew she was young, but I couldn't help myself." Eugene could not stop laughing.

"Your girl goes off herself with another hooker?"

"Yeah, there's a girl there she really likes, I guess. It kind of freaked me out."

"I can understand that. What happened afterwards? Did you guys talk about it?"

"A little. She told me some stuff I can't repeat, but in a way, I guess she invited me to be a more integral part of her life."

"That's a good thing, right? That's what you want isn't it?"

"I thought so, but now I'm not so sure."

We continued talking for a while. I told Eugene about her house, the monkeys and iguanas we saw, the pool, the Haitian art on the walls which particularly interested him. We talked about the rest of the time Ariella and I spent together which was mostly good. As we finished up our food, I thought about what I had not told Eugene, wondering what I was going to do about things with Ariella.

Thirty-three
Hermosa Beach

For the first time in weeks Fred showed up for volleyball. He got picked for Lindsay's team and characteristically he blew a couple of kills that resulted in them losing. At Patrick Molloy's afterward she made sure to grab the seat next to him. They both ordered Bloody Marys and helped themselves from the huge plate of nachos someone ordered. "It's been a while, Fred. What you been up to?" she asked him.

"Well, I've kinda been dating this girl and we took a trip together to Panama."

"Panama," she said, ignoring the knot in her stomach. "What's that like?"

"Oh, you know, tropical, real hot, jungle and stuff. We went to Panama City. That was nice, good restaurants, some clubs and things. It was fun."

"So, this girl, you and she are getting pretty serious?"

"Hard to say, she's pretty complicated. I've never met anyone quite like her. I guess it's up to me to decide if the relationship is going to the next level. She needs me to make some decisions."

Hearing this Lindsay decided to unload what she knew on Fred. Maybe it wouldn't make any difference but she wasn't sure when she would next see Fred and she was worried about him.

"The girl you are seeing is named Ariella Blumkin. I went to high school with her, at least I was a freshman when she was a senior at Leuzinger High."

"How could you have any idea who I'm seeing?"

"By sheer coincidence I happened to be walking by your place one day when she pulled up to pick you up."

"How do you even know where my place is?" Lindsay gulped hard. This was going to be harder than she imagined.

"I didn't. I was just walking down Third Street to the beach from a friend's house when I saw you. I saw her gray Camry pull up. I recognized her from school. I didn't know her but she was so strikingly pretty everyone knew who she was. Fred, she was a little weird."

"I know she's weird, Lindsay, but it's also weird that you know so much about who I am dating."

"No Fred, I mean there's something sinister about her. She has a strange past. Her mother, grandfather and brother were murdered when she was in Junior College. It may have unhinged her. She beat up another girl in high school in front of everyone, really brutally took her down. She had no friends and everyone was sort of afraid of her. That's what I mean by 'sinister.'" Lindsay blurted all this out without taking a breath. She looked over at Fred whose face was frozen.

"Anything else you can tell me?" he asked sarcastically.

"I just think you should know what you are getting yourself into with this girl. Yeah, she's really pretty but she's really strange, Fred, and not in a good way. You need to be careful."

It occurred to Fred that he had been careful all his life and what had it gotten him?

"I appreciate the warning, Lindsay. I agree she's an unusual person, not like anyone I've ever met before. There's some real chemistry between us. Hey, maybe I'm a little weird, too?"

Lindsay sighed and sat back in her chair sipping her Bloody Mary.

"You are a little weird, Fred but not in the same way. I mean aside from the fact this girl is way out of your league, no offense but you know it's true, she's likely to break your heart. Don't you feel like she's potentially dangerous? If she could beat up a classmate in front of the whole school, if she could have her whole family massacred and not blink an eye or shed a tear, what might she be capable of?"

"You don't know her at all, Lindsay. Neither one of us knows what she might be capable of, I suppose. She and I have a relationship. In the end, I guess I just trust her." He finished his drink and got up. "Look, Lindsay, thanks for your concern, but whatever you may have heard about her, I think you've got her wrong."

He got up and left the restaurant.

Thirty-four
J. Edgar Hoover Building, Washington D.C.

Terry Melton was a forensic accountant Diaz assigned to review the information regarding the Tsi, Beckworth and Talisman murders. He was a diminutive figure in his early fifties with gray hair, long sideburns and a thick gray walrus mustache. His customary work clothes were baggy khakis, a white long-sleeved dress shirt and a solid colored tie. Today's version was royal blue.

"We know Jonathon Parsons shipped out two hundred thousand dollars to a numbered account with Crofton's bank in the Cayman Islands," he told Diaz as they sat in a conference room at FBI headquarters. "Money was also wired there by Mrs. Abigail Tsi and James Beckworth. Each of those accounts was a separate numbered account with the same bank."

"I thought Cayman Islands accounts were supposed to be secret. How did we find out the owner of these accounts?"

"We made a request of Crofton's based on suspected criminal activity associated with the account." Melton shuffled the papers in front of him glancing down at them as he spoke. "In recent years, changes in our banking laws as well as international rules have made it increasingly difficult for most offshore banks to maintain absolute secrecy. Cayman banks are now responsive when we can show a link to potential criminal activity. Usually it's tax fraud, but in this case, it was murder for hire and the records from Parson's, Tsi's and Beckworth's banks raised the likelihood these payments to Crofton's accounts were for a hired killer. Crofton's supplied us with the answers which, surprisingly, all led to the same owner, Medusa, S.A., a corporation registered in Panama."

"How do we know anything about Medusa, S.A.?"

"Well, we really shouldn't. Panamanian law provides secrecy protections for the ownership of Panamanian corporations. Even the identity of the shareholders is confidential." Here Melton's voice quickened. "We have been working with the IRS for the last few years since the Panama Papers came out and created a scandal. We have informers in a number of the major Panamanian law firms that cater to foreigners trying to escape their countries' tax laws. We happened to have an informer at Benedict, Alfaro, and Sabredo, the law firm representing Medusa. She told us all of the shares of Medusa, S.A. were owned by a trust and the beneficiary of that trust, also represented by the same law firm, was a woman named Maria Guisado who may also be the trustee. We're not too sure about that. However, we've just found out there have been some changes."

"How so?"

"Maria Guisado is no longer the beneficiary of the trust. Instead, another Panamanian corporation, Voin, S.A., is. We don't know much about Voin. It may not have been formed by Benedict, Alfaro, and Sabredo, so we have no idea who owns it."

"Maria Guisado?"

"We cannot find a thing about this woman other than a few records of her exiting the United States and entering Panama," said Melton, raising his eyebrows. "Panamanian banking rules are very protective, so we have no idea if she has any bank accounts. As far as we can tell, there are no credit cards issued to her and she owns no vehicles or real property."

"She does have a passport, right?" Diaz asked between sips of Cuban coffee.

"She does, a Panamanian passport. The picture on it is pretty blurry but it describes her as twenty-seven years old, five foot seven inches tall with dark hair and blue eyes."

"That could be anybody. Not really helpful at all. Do we have any idea about the activity from the Cayman accounts?"

"Most of the funds pass through the accounts pretty quickly, probably to Panamanian accounts controlled by Medusa, S.A. but we can't be sure and have no way of finding out. It does appear that a significant amount of money has passed through these accounts."

"How much?"

"More than a million dollars over the last twelve months."

"Is there any way to see if some of this money made its way back to the States?" Diaz buzzed for an assistant to refill his coffee.

"So far we can't trace it beyond Panama and we don't know where it went in Panama. It may be that whoever is behind this operation is keeping their money in Panama. Maybe they are Colombians who worked for the cartels who have branched out to do murder for hire. Maybe they somehow have laundered it to send it back to the U.S." Melton sighed. "We're working on it but it is very hard to trace money out of Panama, especially if it's in increments of less than ten thousand dollars."

"Does the fact that they changed trust beneficiaries tell us they are on to us?"

"Possibly," nodded Melton. "It does suggest they may have turned our source within the law firm which is going to make it even harder to trace the money. We'll keep trying."

"Well, let us know if you find anything else out. Our progress in these cases so far is slow. Keep on digging on Maria Guisado. There has to be more on her than just passport information." Melton gathered his papers and left. Diaz was left to ponder exactly what he was dealing with. Was this a murder for hire organization as Melton speculated? Was it just a few individuals who were highly organized and efficient? How had the people who benefitted from these murders found the person to hire? Diaz knew there was one person he had access to who could tell him: that was Jonathon Parsons.

Thirty-five
Hermosa Beach

I had to admit I was disturbed by what Lindsay told me, though maybe not for the reasons she suspected. Ariella mentioned her family were all dead but she hadn't said anything about a murder.

After what she said to me in Panama, I couldn't help but wonder if she was the person who killed her family. I felt guilty even thinking that about someone who meant so much to me. I still had a hard time believing she was capable of killing anyone despite what she told me.

Ariella explained the people she killed were all bad people who deserved it and what she was doing was really just a kind of vigilante justice. Somehow that did not sound right.

The thing is, I cared about Ariella. She was the most beautiful and amazing woman I ever knew. The fact she was interested in me at all was incredible. Of course, she wanted something from me. Isn't that the way relationships work? Not that I'm an expert, but isn't there supposed to be give and take, compromise on both sides? I mean, Ariella paid for everything, she was this scintillating beauty who could have any man she wanted but she chose me. Shouldn't I expect to compromise in some way? Wasn't she just asking for a sort of commitment anyone who cared about her would be willing to give?

The thing is, what she was asking of me went against everything I believed in. I could never even imagine murdering someone. Clearly it was wrong to take a life.

Somehow, she expected me to help her do just that. Even if I wasn't the one pulling the trigger, something I could never do, being part of a plan to take someone's life seemed profoundly wrong. There was the possibility of getting caught, going to jail for decades, maybe even the rest of my life. I've always been an honest person. I don't cheat my clients or overbill them. I never shoplifted or got into fights. I haven't even had many traffic tickets in my life. Was I now going to change who I was just for a strange and beautiful woman?

After she announced to me, she was a hired killer, things went pretty well in Panama.

At first, I was freaked out, didn't know how to deal with it but she let it go for the rest of the trip. We mostly spent time by the pool drinking champagne and hiking in the forest. It rained most afternoons about three. We would usually retreat to the bedroom while the rain pounded on the tile roof, thunder rumbling in the background. After so much champagne and sex, I sort of forgot what she had said about killing people. It seemed like a dream and she never brought it up again herself.

Before we parted at LAX on the way home, she said pointedly, "We are going to need to talk soon."

Since then I had not heard from her and it had been almost three weeks since I last saw her. I wondered if she gave up on me or if the whole thing had been some weird fantasy that only seemed real. Of course, she went incognito for weeks at a time before. Anyway, would she have abandoned me after telling me her secret?

Of course, I had no details about any actual victims and even had I gone to the police would have had nothing of substance to give them to even suggest she committed a crime. Still, for a woman so intent on being invisible she revealed a lot of things about her life to me. Of course, maybe she had never been serious about what she said. Maybe it was some sort of droll joke she played on the infatuated boyfriend. It did seem unlikely this cool, beautiful, elegant, sophisticated woman could do anything as brutal as murder someone, didn't it?

It was Sunday night and I was just sitting at home nursing a Corona when my cell phone rang. I didn't recognize the number it displayed so I assumed it was just a solicitation call but I answered it anyway. "Hey Fred, how are you?"

"I'm good, Ariella. It's been a while since I've heard from you.

Frankly I wasn't sure if I would."

"Now Fred, you know I get busy and focus on the project at hand. Maybe things can change. That's up to you: entirely up to you. Why don't we get together at my place next weekend? You know, the usual arrangement? We can have that talk and see where things are going with us. Okay?"

"I'd love to see you, so yeah let's do that," I said, swallowing hard and feeling nervous about what was to come.

"Great, Fred, I'll pick you up at seven on Friday night, pack a bag."

"Okay, Ariella. I love you," I said, taking a chance on saying it.

"I know, Fred," she said and hung up.

Thirty-six
FBI Regional Headquarters, 26 Federal Plaza, New York City

It was the worst day of Jonathon Parson's life. His office had been invaded by a squadron of FBI agents who drew guns on him, cuffed him and read him his rights. He was told he was being arrested for the murders of Jesse Blake and Paul Voca. He tried to explain that he had alibis for these two murders as he had previously explained to Agent Diaz. As they walked him out of his office, he told his secretary to call his lawyer and get him the best criminal defense lawyer he knew.

He was now sitting in an interrogation room in the FBI regional headquarters in Manhattan. He was cuffed to a table in a room which had four chairs and a single door in which there was a square mirrored window. The floor was linoleum tile and the furniture painted metal. The room felt warm and Parsons could feel himself sweating profusely. It had been almost a half an hour, he guessed, since they placed him in the room. No one looked in on him.

He tried to imagine what they might have on him that would have let them think they could arrest him. He explained the wire transfers and wiped his computer clean of the e-mails to Medusa199. His lawyer knew little and, in any case, would never have talked and the fixer who referred him to Medusa199 knew nothing specific. Anyway, how could they have found out about him?

Finally, Agent Diaz entered the room with two cups in hand. He was dressed in a crisp light blue cotton shirt with dark blue red striped tie and blue gabardine slacks. He looked relaxed and cheerful. He placed a paper cup with a clear bubbly liquid in front of Parsons.

"It's 7-Up," he said, "to calm your stomach. I would imagine right now you are pretty frightened and upset."

"Well, I haven't done anything so I'm having a hard time understanding how you could arrest me for two murders, one of a man I have never even met."

"You do understand you don't have to talk to me without your lawyer present? They read you your Miranda rights when they picked you up, didn't they? I understand there is a lawyer on the way."

"Look, I don't mind talking to you, I have nothing to hide. If I can help in any way to solve these murders, I will."

"You must have something to hide because you have already lied to us once about the purpose for wiring the two hundred thousand to an offshore account."

"I told you I was anticipating some profit taking on the tender offer by Talisman and I was beginning to salt some money away to avoid taxes."

"The account you sent the money to is owned by a corporation that has been linked to money paid for other murders, seven of them to be precise. That two hundred thousand was not an investment: it was payment of a hired killer to take care of your problem with Talisman. That much we can prove."

The door to the room opened and Becky Haden entered with a middle-aged woman in a gray suit. She had gray hair in a short bob, a pearl necklace and a cream-colored blouse. She carried an ox blood leather briefcase.

"I'm Susan Martin, I'll be representing Mister Parsons. Can you tell me about the basis for his arrest?"

"We were just discussing that before you came in. By the way, your client was cautioned he didn't have to speak until you got here and so far, he has said nothing other than to deny the charges. Let me briefly summarize what we have against Mister Parsons. His company was in the process of being acquired in a tender offer by Talisman Management. We have it on strong authority that the plan was to replace the company management after obtaining a controlling interest. That meant your client would be ousted as CEO of the company he founded. Not long after the tender offer was initiated, Jesse Blake, a key employee of Talisman, and Paul Voca, its principal, were murdered. Just prior to the first murder, Mister Parsons wired one hundred thousand dollars to a numbered Cayman Islands account. Just after the second murder he sent another one hundred thousand to that same account. The murders effectively halted the tender offer and Mister Parsons continues as the CEO. He claimed the money was wired in anticipation of profit-taking from the tender offer, even though the second payment was after the death of Paul Voca, which must have pretty clearly indicated the tender offer was no longer on the table. However, we have discovered the Cayman account is actually owned by a Panamanian corporation which also owned accounts for which payments related to several other murders were made. We believe these payments by Mister Parsons were made to engage a professional killer, possibly the same killer as in these other cases."

"I see," said Martin. "And that's the basis of your case against my client?"

"There may have been some other incentive for Mister Parsons to have wanted Blake and Voca out of the way. At this point, we are more interested in finding the actual killer in these and the other murders. If Mister Parsons can provide us with useful information that leads to the identity of the killer, we are inclined to go easy on him."

"Can we have the room for about fifteen minutes so I can confer with my client?" asked Martin.

"Of course," said Diaz as he and Haden got up. Both left the room.

"Mister Parsons, it looks as if they have enough on you to begin digging a lot deeper. What did they not tell me just now?"

"Blake threatened to oust me when they got control unless I resigned. He said if I didn't resign, they would release a statement my ex-wife made in my divorce that I molested my daughter. I couldn't let that happen."

"Okay, what would your wife say now if she were called to testify?"

"I assume she would admit it was false. She did it just to get custody and full child support."

"If she did that, she would be admitting to perjury. Would she do that for you now?"

"To be honest, I'm not sure. We are on much better terms now but I don't know if she would risk admitting perjury to keep me out of jail."

"Even if she did, there is no assurance it would. They have a circumstantial case against you that is not ironclad, but it could result in a conviction. What can you give them?"

"I can give them the name of the fixer who told me about this e-mail and I can give them the e-mail address I used to contact the person they really want to get."

"It's not a lot but it might buy us a reduced charge, maybe even a plea bargain."

"I honestly did not know that the solution to my problems with Talisman was to murder people. When I contacted this e-mail address, no one told me it was a professional killer and no one ever mentioned murder."

"They never do. It's always shorthand. Do you still have the e-mails between you and this person?"

"Medusa199. No, I erased them all from my laptop."

"They can be recovered. By now they will have searched your condo and taken the laptop into custody. They may be able to recover those e-mails from your hard drive. If there was no mention of murder in any of them by either party, maybe we can use your professed ignorance to construct a defense. You've never done anything like this before, have you?"

"Of course not."

"Okay, we don't plead, we try offering what you know for a reduced charge. We argue you had no clue what you were getting yourself into. You never intended for anyone to get hurt."

"Doesn't the fact I paid two hundred thousand dollars kind of mitigate against that argument?"

"Some, but you were desperate, about to lose everything. They promised results, right?"

"That they did, virtually guaranteed them."

"Okay I think we're ready to deal."

Martin got up and went to the door opened it and indicated to Diaz and Haden to come back in. With them was a thin African American woman from the District Attorney's office.

"We can offer you a contact and an e-mail address," said Martin after they all sat down at the table. "What does that buy us?"

Thirty-seven
San Pedro, California

It went like it always had the three or four times I had gone to her house for a weekend. She picked me up in Hermosa in her dusty gray Camry, which never seemed to get washed, and drove us down to the harbor to her white brick warehouse. As always, the craftsman bungalows lined First Street as we passed through a series of stop signs heading down toward the harbor. These elegant little wood-frame homes had been occupied by working class families for almost a century. Now they were worth seven to eight hundred thousand each and the neighborhood would inevitably change. Ariella didn't say much as she drove. She did greet me warmly and hugged me when she picked me up. I found myself looking around to see if Lindsay was somewhere spying on me.

We picked up dinner on the way to the warehouse, tacos and burritos at the little place on the corner of First and Pacific. Ariella ordered me to go to the kitchen and crack open a bottle of Roederer and bring it back to the sitting area where we would eat.

She put on an Art Pepper album I recognized as "Smack Up" with Jack Sheldon on trumpet. We listened as we ate. Ariella held the glass of Roederer up and watched the light filter through the bubbles.

It didn't take long to kill the bottle. I cleaned up the remains of dinner and got another bottle from the kitchen while Ariella put on a Chet Baker record. It was early Chet with him singing sad songs like "Everything Happens To Me," "I've Never Been In Love Before," "My Funny Valentine" and "But Not For Me." His soft, sad, melodic voice and the mournful trumpet solos between vocals settled us down, softened the mood.

Pretty soon we were making out. Each kiss from her was like being shocked by an electric eel. My body filled with the current and I wanted to explode. She let my hands explore her body and I became powerfully aroused. Any moment I expected her to lead me up to her bedroom to let the real fun, and pain, begin.

Instead her eyes suddenly opened between kisses as if they had been powered on. Those huge electric blue eyes could be scary sometimes and they were scary now. There was an intensity that was overwhelming. "Have you thought about my invitation?"

"You mean…?"

"Yes, my invitation to join me, to work with me, to be with me?"

"You're asking me to help you commit crimes." I sensed her tensing up when I said that.

"Is that a 'no,' Fred?"

"I love you, Ariella."

"That's still not an answer. This is who I am, Fred. Rules mean nothing to me. Other people's lives mean nothing to me. I do exactly what I want with no guilt or regrets."

"Don't you ever get afraid of getting caught?"

"No, I don't get caught. I commit murders that other people have motives for, I cover my tracks carefully, I live well under the radar. Officially, I barely exist. Now you understand why I live the way I do, why I have multiple identities and even drive an unobtrusive, unglamorous car."

"Doesn't it bother you that you are hurting people, robbing them of their lives as if you were their judge and jury, like you are playing god?"

"In this world, Fred, there are predators and prey. Some of us are gifted, superior. We have the right to exercise our powers. The rules of the others don't apply to us."

"That goes against everything I have ever been taught. I just am not comfortable with the idea. I don't know."

Ariella seemed to tense up as she heard this. A strange, hard look came into those huge blue eyes, her fists clenched and her mouth tightened. I wondered if this meant she was afraid of losing me.

In fact, I could not bear losing her. What had my life been up to this point? I was isolated, alone. My life was meaningless, pointless, futile. I did not believe in God so I was not afraid of divine retribution. Throwing in my lot with Ariella did not mean throwing away my life. It meant a new beginning, a new way of seeing things, a chance to be with the most beautiful, compelling girl I had ever met.

"I love you," I said. "I want nothing more than to be with you. I'll do whatever you want."

She visibly relaxed and smiled what passed for a genuine smile. I could only infer she cared enough for me to have felt real anxiety about my answer.

"I'm so glad, Fred. We have a lot to talk about. I want you to close your practice down and come live with me."

"What about my condo?"

"Sell it, lease it, whatever, you won't need it."

She leaned over and kissed me hard on the lips. With Ariella kisses always turned into something more painful, that was alright, it was alright with me.

I spent Saturday helping her clean up her place. We took a walk along Cabrillo beach and had dinner at a Croatian restaurant.

That night we watched a Luis Buñuel film, *Belle de Jour*, while killing several bottles of champagne. As usual, Ariella showed no signs of being affected by the alcohol. No one mentioned the discussion of the night before and I wondered if any of it had been serious.

That night I staggered up to her bedroom. When we got there, she stripped naked and proceeded to repeatedly slap me with conviction. I dropped to my knees and she walked around me to put my hands in restraints then dragged me to the bed. It pretty much went downhill from there.

The next morning, released from my restraints I fixed her a mushroom omelet with sourdough toast and a mimosa made from fresh-squeezed orange juice.

"Nice job, Fred," she told me. "I'm happy to report I have a new project for us to collaborate on. You need to clear your calendar for the week after next, we'll be going to Chicago for a week."

"You mean you have a victim?" I asked.

"I have a client who needs to have someone eliminated, so that's what we'll do."

"Does it really take a week to 'eliminate' someone?"

"There is a great deal of planning that goes into a project like this. That is, if you don't want to get caught. The first thing we need to do is to ensure we have weapons. Come with me."

She slipped on a robe and we took the elevator down to the forbidden basement level. We entered the gun room and Ariella pulled out a drawer with seven identical automatic pistols.

"These are Beretta 92FS compacts, a nine-millimeter pistol. I stole a case of these from a gun dealer in Barstow several years ago and these are what I have left. I've filed the serial number off each one so they can't be traced. I only use a weapon once, Fred, then I dispose of it as efficiently as possible. Even if one of these beauties were found it would not be connected to any other crime and would be completely untraceable."

She picked one of the jet-black pistols out of the drawer and grabbed two thirteen-round magazines from a second drawer along with a small box of ammunition from a rack by the wall. She pulled out a small shipping box and filled it with packing material before dropping the pistol, magazines and ammunition in. she went to another drawer and pulled out a long, black, metal tube.

"It's an Osprey nine-millimeter silencer," she told me, "and, as a special treat, let me add one of these," she said, dropping a gleaming, stainless steel switchblade into the box. "You never know just what kind of weapon circumstances require. I have to admit I prefer using the knife. It's messy but quiet and it gives me a wonderful sense of triumph when I see the blood flow. I'll ship this box via UPS to a commercial postal center in Chicago where we'll pick it up since we obviously can't climb on a plane with this hardware."

She finished sealing the box and affixed an address label she had already printed.

"The box will get there before we do. The purpose in giving ourselves some time is to evaluate the victim. Find out what her habits are and when she is most likely to be vulnerable, you know, just get the lay of the land. This will be an easy one, Fred. The girl has no security, she's a graduate student. She lives alone and goes back and forth to school. I'm only getting seventy-five thousand for this one, Fred, but it's a perfect project for you to get broken in on."

"What did this girl do to deserve being hunted down by a hired killer?"

"She made a big mistake, Fred: she got pregnant."

Thirty-eight
Hyde Park Neighborhood, Chicago, Illinois

She always enjoyed the walk back to her apartment from campus. The tree lined, leafy streets and the old brownstone town houses were lovely. Their beauty belied the fact that the neighborhood could sometimes be dangerous. But now, in mid-afternoon, she felt safe since the streets were filled with students going back and forth between their apartments and the University of Chicago. As she walked, she could not help but think about the future and the man who had become so important to her.

The previous summer she worked for the reelection campaign of Congressman Mario Furuta. He was the most handsome man Ramona ever met, half Italian, half Japanese with jutting cheekbones, jet black hair and bright amber eyes like those of a jungle cat. He was immensely charming, highly intelligent and full of restless energy.

When it became clear he wanted to seduce her she gave in without hesitation, even though she knew he had a wife and two young children. He was thirty-seven but he had more energy than any man her own age she had ever dated. They had been lovers ever since, discreetly and quietly. He had been easily reelected and now spent most of his time in Washington. He still managed to see her whenever he was in town.

Ramona Baxter was a doctoral candidate in political science at the University of Chicago. At twenty-two she had a fresh, wholesome beauty with long auburn hair, bright blue eyes and a creamy complexion. She would not have been out of place on the cover of a corn flakes box or an ad for women's skin care products. She was certain being pregnant with

Mario's child enhanced her inner glow.

After a twenty-minute walk she arrived at her second story studio apartment in an old brownstone townhouse. She felt a bit dizzy from the walk. She was only ten weeks pregnant but it was already beginning to show a little. She was already beginning to feel the effects. She got very tired at night and she had just started to have morning sickness. Once she really began to show, she suspected she would no longer have to fend off advances from the many male grad students who were always hitting on her.

Unfortunately, Mario had not been as excited about the baby as she was. He wanted her to have an abortion, something she would never do. He offered to pay for the procedure, even to send her on a vacation to the Caribbean or Mexico. She was determined to have the baby.

She knew it was a terrible cliché to be the "other woman" pressuring her man to divorce his wife and marry her. That was exactly what she wanted. Mario had not initially been enthusiastic about this proposal but she knew he did not want to stop seeing her. She planned on using every bit of leverage she had to get what she wanted for herself and their child.

Mario campaigned on family values. His wife and two young daughters frequently made campaign appearances with him. In the blue-collar Catholic district he represented, an affair and divorce might not go over well. He had plans to eventually run for a senate seat and the breath of scandal attached to having a mistress could be an obstacle.

She understood all that. She told him if they worked together to present a united front and tell everyone how much they loved each other it would be far preferable to her going public with the affair on her own, simply portraying him as a man who cheated on his wife but did not stand by his lover either. Mario reluctantly agreed. His preference would be to discreetly divorce his wife. After the divorce was final, he would bring Ramona out into the open. She knew he would eventually come around and she was perfectly capable of being patient. The baby might have come at an awkward time for both of them, but by the time it was born she would be happily situated as Mrs. Mario Furuta, wife of the future United States senator from Illinois.

Thirty-nine
J. Edgar Hoover Building, Washington, D.C.

Efforts to get anything out of the "fixer," whose name Jonathon Parsons gave them, proved futile. He denied ever having had the conversation with Parsons and any knowledge of the Medusa199 e-mail. They only had Parsons' word to contradict him so they stopped pursuing him and decided to use the e-mail address to set a trap for the hit man.

Diaz referred the e-mail address to the FBI's technical specialists to try to trace its origins. However, as Diaz suspected, the Russian company sponsoring Medusa's e-mail was uncooperative. Attempts to digitally trace the origins of the e-mail address found it bouncing between servers all over Eastern Europe and Latin America. Tracing its origin would be impossible so a trap was the only option.

The problem with setting a trap was, who would be the decoy? Whoever that was would be in real danger no matter how carefully they set up security. Any trap would require a potential victim and a substantial prepayment. The situation had to appear real enough for the killer to act.

Diaz came up with the idea to ask the killer to assassinate a dignitary visiting from a foreign country. They could set up the trap in a hotel in New York. He had the IT section set up an e-mail address and sent Medusa199 a message:

Pablo Corrales, Assistant Foreign Minister of Argentina has become a political liability. We request help in dealing with this problem. He will be in New York City on the twenty-second through the twenty-fourth of next month for a United Nations Committee meeting. Perhaps you can arrange a meeting with him then?

137

Within forty-five minutes they received a response.

The problem can be solved. A fee of two hundred thousand dollars will be required. Please wire initial payment of one hundred thousand dollars to Chandler's Bank, Cayman Islands Account number 300297458766654. Remainder of the fee is due upon solution of the problem. Please send information regarding his arrival and departure times, dates. Identify where he will be staying while in New York.

The trap was set. Corrales would be played by Special Agent Ed Sanchez who would be booked into the Millennium Hilton on U.N. Plaza. He would be shadowed at all times by undercover agents and wear a bulletproof vest under his suit. As soon as the killer made a move, a half dozen armed agents would be on top of him.

The initial problem, Diaz knew, would be getting authorization to wire one hundred thousand dollars to the killer. This money would melt away into the ethos, and even if the killer were caught, might never be recovered. The trick would be to convince the Assistant Director in charge of his unit that this was a big enough bust to merit risking one hundred thousand dollars. In addition, there would be costs for booking a decent enough hotel room to convince the killer this was a real Argentinian diplomat and activating a team of agents to provide security around the clock for Sanchez.

Diaz met with his boss, Assistant Director Patricia Patterson, a tired, bored-looking, white middle-aged woman who had worked her way through the agency over a twenty-seven-year career. "So, Agent Diaz, you think you have a professional assassin in your net?"

"We're close, Director. We just need some bait to sweeten the trap and we should have him. So far we've linked this killer to six deaths in New York and three in Singapore but it's pretty likely he can be linked to other killings."

"Is this an organization we're talking about or a single individual acting alone?"

"We don't know for sure. My personal guess is it's an organization. There is a Latin American connection that may be more than just a coincidence. It's possible this is a group of former or present cartel members who have branched out into murder for hire. Obviously, we'll know a lot more once we get our hands on the killer."

"How certain are you that you can pull this off?"

"We've already had a response from the killer's e-mail. All we need to set the plan in motion is to pay the initial one hundred-thousand-dollar fee and we are off to the races."

Diaz looked up at the Assistant Director hopefully and to gage her response to the mention of the money. She stared back at him expressionless. They sat there awkwardly for two or three minutes before she finally responded.

"You have a go. Diaz, you have a great reputation within the agency. You've pulled off some high-profile arrests so I'm taking a chance on this one. It's a lot of money to front in an investigation. It's an operation that will require a lot of resources and potentially put an agent at risk. If you don't pull it off, there will be a significant black mark against you. Is that understood?"

"Yes, Director, I understand the risk."

"Good. I'll authorize finance to advance you the hundred thousand and from here it's your operation, sink or swim."

Diaz had never been afraid of taking risks and he felt that the odds of this operation succeeding were high.

Forty
Hyde Park Neighborhood, Chicago, Illinois

Ariella told me there were to be no cell phones, that I should leave mine at home, so I did. She booked us on a United Airlines flight to Chicago out of LAX. She provided me with a California driver's license under the name of Alan Porter but with a picture of me. Hers was in the name of Helen Porter.

"See, Fred, we're a happily married couple just like you've always wanted us to be," she said, taking my arm as we boarded the plane.

We were in first class but Ariella warned me, "No alcohol during the entire trip, we'll save that for afterward."

When the drink tray came around, I opted for a 7-Up. It was an evening flight and Ariella was asleep almost as soon as we were in the air. I, on the other hand, was kept awake by my own nerves.

Ariella seemed positively chipper about our little expedition but I kept on feeling as if I were making a huge mistake. The whole purpose of our trip was to kill some poor pregnant girl. Was I really doing this? I tried to keep my misgivings from Ariella. I couldn't help a queasy feeling in the bottom of my gut at the thought that what I was doing was wrong and no good would come of it.

We landed at O'Hare about seven thirty in the morning. Just before we landed Ariella opened her eyes and smiled at me. She went from sleep to fully awake faster than anyone I ever knew. She seemed happy and excited in contrast to my sense of gloomy despair.

We only had carry-on luggage so I followed Ariella down through the baggage claim area to the CTA station where we grabbed a train toward the city.

Ariella told me she usually did not rent cars on these trips to avoid leaving any more of a paper trail than was necessary so we would be using public transportation and paying cash wherever we could.

We got off the train at the Jackson Street Station and walked up to street level where we got a number six bus that took us straight to Hyde Park. We got off a block away from the Hyatt Place Chicago-South Hotel by the University Medical Center. Ariella had reserved a modest room in the name of Mr. and Mrs. Alan Porter. "I always try to stay in large, mid-level hotels," she told me, "the kind of places where the guests are anonymous and no one notices you among the crowd."

The Hyatt Place was definitely that kind of place. It was clean, modern, bland and had hundreds of rooms. No one would remember the Porters staying there.

"Ramona Baxter lives in a studio apartment in an old townhouse about six blocks from campus. We start by monitoring her coming and going. We try to find a place and time in her schedule where she will be vulnerable, where no one else is around, but first we need to collect our tools."

We checked in, left our bags in the room, and walked seven blocks to a UPS Store where Ariella presented an ID to the clerk and collected the package she sent from Los Angeles. We took it back to the hotel and opened it.

Ariella checked the barrel of the Beretta to insure it was clean, snapped in a magazine full of cartridges and dropped the loaded gun into her purse. She put the switch blade into the pocket of her jacket and wrapped the remaining magazine, ammunition and the silencer in one of her blouses and stowed it in her suitcase.

We headed into the Hyde Park neighborhood. The streets were lined with leafy green trees and old townhouses from the late nineteenth century. Clearly this had once been a very elegant neighborhood.

"That's her place," said Ariella when we were across the street from a three-story brownstone townhouse. "She lives on the second story. She should be in school now. Let's check the alley while we have time."

We walked to the end of the block and turned into an alley that ran behind the townhouse. In back were trash bins and a metal fire escape that clung to the unpainted brick back of the building.

We strolled the length of the alley and back out onto the street. Students were beginning to make their way back from campus. We lingered on the street and after a while we saw a young woman approaching. She wore jeans and a sweat jacket. As she got closer you could make out her long auburn hair. "That's her," said Ariella.

She carried some books and a notebook. From what I could see of her she looked pretty and sweet and innocent. It did not seem real that we were here tracking her to plot her demise.

We hung around for a while until it got dark, strolling the street and the alley behind the townhouse, trying to stay inconspicuous. She did not emerge from her apartment and finally Ariella said, "Fred, you can't come to Chicago without sampling the deep-dish pizza. Let's go eat."

We went back to the hotel and got a taxi to take us to a little place that was famous for Chicago style pizza and shared a pie. I wasn't that hungry, my appetite affected by the anxiety I felt. Ariella managed to put away three pieces of deep-dish pizza into her slender body and seemed to thoroughly enjoy them. After that we went back to the hotel.

"We'll be up early tomorrow morning to track Ramona to campus and find out where her classes are," Ariella told me. We climbed into bed and turned off the lights. "By the way, Fred, no sex while we are on a project, understood?"

I nodded my head in the dark but it seemed like she was already asleep.

For the next couple of days, we followed Ramona Baxter from her apartment to the University of Chicago campus. She was usually out of her place by nine and walked the few blocks to get to campus. Each day Ariella wore a different wig. Some days she put on a pair of heavy dark rimmed glasses. When I asked her if I should do anything to alter my appearance she said, "No, Fred, you're already as inconspicuous as you can get. I'm not worried she'll notice you."

Ramona Baxter's classes were in a trio of buildings on the Eastern part of the campus. They were old, gothic looking red brick buildings with high peaked roofs and dormer windows. Ariella took a particular interest in each building scouting the hallways and stairways. Ramona's first seminar was in an old three-story building with no elevator but her seminar room was on the ground floor. The other two buildings had single rickety old elevators. Her last class of the day was on the third floor of one of those buildings. Ariella noted that by the time her class was finished, about four in the afternoon, there were few other students in the building. Ramona apparently felt a bit claustrophobic in the old elevator, which every other student in her seminar took to the ground floor after class. She typically went down the back stairs to get out.

Ramona Baxter did little of note with her evenings. Sometimes she went back to campus to use the library. Some nights her lights went off about nine-thirty or ten. She did not seem to go out or to have many friends. She led the lonely, sequestered life of a graduate student.

How, I wondered, had this woman managed to get herself pregnant? There was no sign of any boyfriend, not much interaction between Ramona and other male students. When I expressed curiosity about the father of Ramona's baby Ariella told me I didn't need to know and the less I knew the better.

After three days of following her around, Ariella, as we sat at dinner in a little coffee shop not far from our hotel, said, "I think I've figured out the logistics and we are ready to move. Tomorrow is Thursday and she has her three classes. We'll deal with her after the last class of the day."

The next morning, we did not get up to follow Ramona Baxter from her apartment. Instead we had a leisurely breakfast in the hotel restaurant and went back to our room to pack our bags.

Ariella gave me a pair of latex gloves. She grabbed a red wig and sunglasses. We went down to the front desk to check out and store our bags with the bellman. We spent some time walking by Lake Michigan. Ariella was quiet but calm. We had lunch at an Italian restaurant near the Loop. After lunch Ariella ducked into the restaurant's restroom and emerged a redhead. We took the bus back to Hyde Park and walked to campus.

We sat at a bench close to the building where Ramona Baxter's last class was and pretended to make out. We saw her head to the entrance door at about two-thirty. At about three forty-five we took our places, Ariella lingering in the hall and me at the bottom of the back stairwell Ramona Baxter usually used to leave the building. Ariella showed me how to lock the stairwell doors on the first and second from the inside by pushing up on the bar on the door. I could hear my heart beating and my hands were dripping with sweat inside the latex gloves.

Finally, I heard the door at the top of the stairwell open and footsteps on the stairs. I started up the stairs and, as I reached the landing between the first and second floors, I saw Ramona coming about half way down the stairs between the third and second floors. I glimpsed the red-haired Ariella behind her at the top of the stairwell. Ramona Baxter smiled at me in surprise as she saw me, a smile so sweet and unsuspecting it broke my heart. Before she could say a word, Ariella grabbed her from behind with one hand over her mouth and the other, switchblade in hand, sliced quickly across her throat. I watched in horror as Ariella shoved the now lifeless body down the stairs to the landing. I backed down the stairs to avoid the pool of blood forming there. Ariella leaned over and wiped the switchblade off on Ramona's blouse then quickly hopped over the body. "Let's get out of here," she said quietly. I didn't have to be told twice.

We left the building and walked swiftly off campus. Before we left Ariella ducked into a restroom and removed her wig and reversed the jacket she was wearing. We got back to the hotel and reclaimed our luggage. Ariella went into the lobby bathroom and put together a package including the Beretta she brought with the silencer, clips and ammunition, our latex gloves, the switchblade she used to dispatch Ramona Baxter and the various wigs and glasses she had worn. We walked the several blocks from the hotel to Lake Michigan. Ariella grabbed a few rocks and placed them into the canvas laundry bag with the weapons and wigs. With no one around she hurled the bag into the lake. We walked a while down Lakeshore Drive pulling our carry-ons until we were able to hail a taxi to take us to O'Hare.

At the airport, we found the COPA counter and checked in. Ariella used a Panamanian passport in the name of Juanita DeSantis. I used an American passport in the same name of Alan Porter that Ariella gave me.

I should have been nervous about using a phony passport to get through TSA but I was already so shaken by what I saw that day I didn't really care. Once we were in the terminal Ariella immediately went to the closest bar and ordered a Calvados. I decided I would try one too even though I didn't know what it was. The caramel-colored liquid was smooth and strangely complex but with a nice kick to it. It would take two or three more, however, to numb the horror of watching a sweet, auburn-haired girl get her throat slashed.

Forty-one
J. Edgar Hoover Building, Washington, D.C.

Diaz was scanning a homicide report from across the country at his desk. A murder in Chicago caught his eye. A young, female graduate student had her throat cut in a back stairwell of a building on the campus of the University of Chicago. The Hyde Park neighborhood in which the university was located had its share of crime but there were very few instances of crime of any sort on campus. The methodology of the crime reminded him of the unsolved murder of Maria Amendola in Honduras. The savage use of a knife on the throat of a relatively harmless female victim was common to both but this crime occurred in a place where the victim should have felt safe. To satisfy his curiosity Diaz placed a call to Chicago P.D. Homicide.

He finally got connected to a homicide detective named Achilles Jackson, Jr. "What's the interest of the FBI in a case like this? Girl just got caught in a back stairwell by some creep."

"It bears a slight resemblance to some other cases we're working on. It's probably not related but I thought it was worth following up on just in case. Was anything taken from her, a wallet, jewelry, anything of value?" asked Diaz.

"Her I.D. was on her and she had a few bucks in her wallet. No, didn't look like she got robbed."

"Any forensic evidence?"

"That's what's so weird about this one, no prints, no weapon, no footprints. We dusted everything but it was clean. Whoever did this was very careful. I mean the crime was like a crime of passion or something a psychopath would do but they aren't usually that careful, are they?"

"Some are. Was there anything about this girl that would make you think she might have been a target for a killer? Boyfriend, jilted lover, rival in love, anything like that? Had she done anything to piss anybody off?"

"Not that we know of, but one thing, the girl was pregnant."

"Interesting. Any idea who the father is?"

"No, her friends, people who knew her from school, say they didn't think she had a boyfriend. I talked to the parents this morning. They had no clue she was seeing anyone."

"Of course, the parents are always the last to know at her age, right?"

"True. Whoever it was they did a good job of covering their tracks, must have been a reason the girl kept the relationship under wraps. Look, we'll continue to investigate. I'll let you know if we find anything and hey, if you think you know anything about this let us know, okay?"

"I promise. Just right now, I don't have a thing to connect it to anything we're working on but if something comes up, I'll give you a call. Thanks for your help." Diaz hung up and got back to planning the trap to catch medusa199.

Ed Sanchez would check into the Millennium Hilton as Pablo Corrales of the Argentinian State Department on the twenty-second next month. He would go daily to the United Nations by foot and dine publicly each evening with other FBI agents dressed as foreign officials. Reservations would be made through the hotel concierge. The trick would be to make him seem vulnerable to invite an attack by Medusa199 while still protecting him. One hundred thousand dollars had been wired to a numbered Cayman Islands account. Medusa was e-mailed detailed information regarding the arrival and accommodations of Pablo Corrales. A picture of agent Sanchez dressed as Pablo Corrales was also e-mailed to Medusa1199.

The numbered account to which the funds had been wired was owned by a Panamanian Corporation, Voin, S.A. None of the IRS informers in Panamanian law firms could tell them who owned the corporation and, of course, as Terry Melton explained earlier, information on the shareholders of Panamanian corporations was confidential. If the killer they just hired was the same one who killed Paul Voca and the others, they had changed law firms to set up new corporations. Maybe the medusa199 e-mail was like an exchange of killers for hire and you simply got the next one in the rotation? Diaz hoped not: the chance to get the Voca/Beckworth killer would solve nine homicides. It would be a major coup for his office if he could trap that killer and remove a dangerous predator from the street.

Agent Sanchez was preparing for his role as Pablo Corrales, buying appropriate clothing to look like a diplomat while hiding a bulletproof vest and concealed weapon. Diaz was in the process of getting a team together to provide support and protection twenty-four hours a day while "Pablo Corrales" was in New York.

He established contact with NYPD requesting Becky Haden as their liaison officer for the operation so he could work with someone he knew and trusted. The hotel room had been booked, team meetings already scheduled even before all team members could be identified and the Argentinian delegation to the United Nations had been recruited to supply cover for Agent Sanchez. It was all ready for the window of opportunity to open. Diaz was looking forward to meeting this highly skilled, professional, very brutal killer face to face.

Forty-two
Buena Vista, Panama

Ariella ordered a cognac on the COPA flight and got a spare one for later. I did the same thing. I'm not usually a big consumer of hard liquor but I was still disturbed at what I saw that day, actually, at what I had been a part of. I couldn't get that girl's smile out of my head. It was so trusting and guileless while I was there to make sure she got her throat slit.

Ariella complained about the quality of the cognac and promptly fell asleep after quaffing both miniature bottles. It did taste harsh, bitter, doing little to take the edge off my fear, anxiety and guilt. I sat awake during the entire flight wondering exactly who or what I had become and how I had gotten to this place.

Ariella slept until the wheels went down for the landing at Tocumen airport. When the plane landed, we parted company to go through separate immigration lines, her for residents and me for visitors. We met up after customs and stepped out into the hot, humid air outside the terminal. Somehow Ariella had a car waiting for us. The driver was the same guy who picked me up weeks before. Ariella insisted we stop at a Price Smart, a giant store almost exactly like Costco at home, on the way out of town, to buy steaks for dinner that night.

The ride to Ariella's *casa* was uneventful. I didn't feel much like talking and she, as usual, was calmly quiet. As soon as we got to the house, she tipped the driver and ran inside. She yelled to me to get a bottle of champagne from the fridge and open it. She quickly stripped off all her clothes and plunged into the pool. I grabbed the champagne and two

Riedel crystal flutes, filling them up and bringing them outside to the patio.

"You're not afraid to have glass near the pool?" I asked.

"I never break things unless I intend to, Fred, and it's a crime to drink decent champagne from plastic. Come in, we can celebrate now."

I really felt little like celebrating but I tossed off my clothes and jumped in. The water did feel good, cool in the warm humid air and somehow soothing to my prickly conscience.

Ariella grabbed me in the water and our naked bodies locked together. Her kiss was as electric as ever and I was reminded why I dropped myself into this moral abyss. This girl, so beautiful and electric like no one I had ever encountered, and I wanted her like I never wanted anyone else in my life and damn the cost.

We spent the afternoon swimming and drinking champagne. We went through three bottles in about three hours. While I could still not keep up with Ariella, I was doing better. By the time the sun went down, I was very drunk. We sat on the patio by the pool sipping from our Riedel flutes as a huge yellow moon began to emerge. It was the largest, most imposing moon I ever saw. The sky around it was littered with stars, something we never see in ambient-light-polluted Los Angeles. Here, with no ambient light, the house lights all turned off, the forest dark, the sky glowed like a planetarium dominated by the tropical moon. Suddenly, as I looked up at the sky I began to weep.

"Why Fred, I had no idea you were such a sensitive soul," said Ariella in a mocking voice.

I had no answer so I just sat there in the chaise lounge by the pool weeping quietly.

"I think it's time you grilled the steaks," she said, "and try not to cry on mine. It will make it too salty."

Somehow, I pulled myself together and lit the gas barbecue. I threw the steaks on and put together a simple salad with the stuff we bought at Price Smart.

Ariella went into the house and emerged with a 1985 Pomerol. I wasn't sure I could drink any more but Ariella pulled out two red wine glasses and uncorked the old bottle with quiet efficiency.

We sat at a table out on the patio under the tropical moon eating our steaks and drinking the Pomerol. I was too drunk to appreciate the wine but I noticed Ariella sloshing it around in her glass sniffing it with reverence.

"Are you mourning poor little Ramona Baxter, Fred?" she asked, looking up from her glass of Pomerol.

"I'm not sure. I find her death disturbing and my part in it even more disturbing."

"Ramona Baxter was having an affair with a very prominent married, U.S. congressman with realistic ambitions for a senate seat in the next election. Sweet little Ramona was pregnant with his child despite the fact the congressman says he was very careful about that sort of thing. Do you wonder how that happened, Fred? Ramona was using the pregnancy, which she refused to terminate despite the congressman's offer to pay for everything, as leverage to get him to leave his wife and marry her. The congressman is a Republican, Fred, and in his district a scandal like this would destroy his career. Ramona Baxter was a greedy, selfish, grasping little bitch and now he's rid of her. We did a good thing, Fred, and as a bonus we got paid a lot of money to do it. How can that make you sad?"

I looked at her for a moment trying to figure out if she was really serious. A part of me was beginning to realize Ariella was never serious about anything other than maybe making her kills and collecting her money.

"The congressman was very smart to keep his relationship with Ramona entirely secret. No one suspects him," she continued. "One of my past clients recently got arrested because a very clever FBI agent followed the money from his personal account to my off-shore account and they linked that account with my corporation which received money from other suspects in other cases. Really Fred, there's no privacy anymore. Apparently, the fool lied about the reason for sending the money off-shore and he started talking. My law firm in Panama City developed a leak and one of my favorite aliases got outed. So, I've changed a lot of things up, left that law firm, set up new corporations and started using another level of Panamanian corporations as trustees. The more firewalls the better, right, Fred? I'm also instructing future clients to establish their own off-shore accounts and transfer the money to my accounts from their accounts. Their ownership of the accounts will be revealed to the U.S. government but not the details of any transactions so that should protect them. Of course, I've started using another alias, one that's not associated with any of my trusts or corporations. I'm now Juanita DeSantis. Pretty sexy, huh, Fred? Okay, no secrets, right? I've just told you everything that's going on with me, now you tell me how you're really feeling?"

Ariella didn't usually say a lot, so all this talking was surprising. The stuff about the corporations and off-shore accounts was just confusing to me as drunk as I was. I didn't know what to say. I was not feeling good and not feeling like myself. "I'm okay," I said.

"I don't think so, Fred. I don't think so at all."

Later she asked me about my plans to close my practice, lease or sell my condo. I just gave her ambiguous answers. These were things I had not thought much about and now seemed increasingly unlikely to happen. I wasn't sure about anything.

That night she made love to me as savagely as she ever had. She bit my neck, drew blood, slapped me until my face was bruised and red, choked me until I was insensate. It was for me a troubled night. I awakened in the morning badly bruised and hung over. I put on a pair of shorts and staggered downstairs. Ariella was standing by the pool looking down at the tree line at the bottom of the hill. She had a glass of champagne in her hand. "Look, Fred, monkeys." Sure, enough there was a whole troop of Capuchin monkeys, maybe fifteen or twenty, playing in the tree tops.

"When I see them, I always feel it's a good omen," she said. "A kind of affirmation."

I couldn't tell how drunk she was but it seemed like a strange thing to say, even for her.

"The monkeys are an affirmation?" I asked. "An affirmation of what exactly?"

"Of what I do, of who I am. They emerge from the forest and reveal themselves to me like a gift, like they're saying they are happy with me. Make breakfast, Fred. The coffee's already made."

I threw together a couple of omelets, some local sausages, toast with the marmalade she liked. The monkeys were gone. As we sat there on the patio by the pool, I couldn't help myself, I had to ask the question I had been fidgeting with for days. "Your family, they were murdered right? While you were in Junior College?"

"Yes Fred," she answered quietly. "Each one of them had their throat slit."

"Did you, did you…?"

"Fred, you know the answer to that question. Why did you even bother asking?" she said gently and sadly as if speaking to a stubborn child.

I realized that of course, she was right, I knew the answer, had known it since Lindsay talked about the killings. I made the decision then and there that I was through with Ariella. I would finish our holiday together, fly back to L.A., go home and never see her again. I would go on with my life just as I had been before I met her. I was a fool, I knew that and perhaps I had known it from the beginning but it was over now, over for good.

I went into the kitchen after we finished to clean up and load the dishes into the dishwasher. As I rinsed and scraped, I felt a presence behind me. "So, Fred, you're leaving me?"

"I never said that."

"That's not a denial. You are, aren't you?"

"Well, I don't think I can live this way. I'm sorry but I don't think I ever understood who you were."

She laughed as I said this.

"Of course, you didn't, Fred. What you saw was a beautiful woman, not a person. You were dazzled. I spotted you a mile away, Fred."

"What do you mean?"

"I mean, I saw who you were right away in that bar in Chinatown like you gave off an aura. A submissive, unattached, white male with low self-esteem and moderate intelligence. Did you never wonder why this beautiful, rich woman just fell into your lap, Fred? You knew it wasn't because of your irresistible charms. You were useful to me, Fred, at least I hoped you would be. You have to admit that sexually our tastes mesh very nicely. The fly in the old ointment turned out to be that conscience of yours. How boring, how droll. Killing some chiseling little slut gets you all teary eyed. I would have thought a lawyer might be a tad more mercenary than that. After all, Fred, that easy little killing made us a cool seventy-five thousand dollars and that's money we don't bother to pay taxes on. I live the way I do because I don't let petty, moral quibbles get in the way of what I need to do. Fred, I killed my family when I was nineteen because they were a burden. My mother treated me like I needed a chastity belt. I had no freedom, she was overbearing. My brother was a burden, he couldn't function on his own. He could never hold a job, barely made it through school. I wasn't going to put up with either one of them for the rest of my life, they were like stones chained to my leg. My grandfather, well, he was just there, so he had to go, too. When they were gone there was cash and I could sell the condo and it helped put me through UCLA, made my life much easier. Oh, that professor I had the affair with I told you about on our first romantic date? I killed him too. He was trying to dump me, go back to his wife and child. Like you, Fred, he felt guilty about what we were doing. You know what, Fred? All those killings, they felt good. They gave me a sense of power and freedom I never knew before. I could take a life, that's the ultimate power. It's when I realized that was what I wanted. I wanted to be free and rich. I wanted to kill people, hurt them as badly as I could. So, the perfect job for me was professional assassin, right, Fred? It took a while but I established myself, made contacts, got referrals. As time went by, I developed a reputation and my fee went up. I got to pick and choose my targets. I went for the high-profile ones, the ones that paid the best. So, I'm sorry, Fred."

"I know, Ariella, I'm sorry too. I'm sorry it didn't work out."

"No, Fred, I meant I'm sorry I have to kill you." It was then that she pulled a Beretta from the pocket of her robe and pointed it at me. "You know too much. Hell, you know everything. I can't have you walking around out there. You're a huge liability."

I suddenly realized that a relationship with Ariella was like a relationship with a panther: it might be sleek and lovely but it could turn on you at any time, it was incredibly deadly.

"Please, Ariella." I was weeping again this time out of sheer terror.

"I won't say a word to anyone, really. I do care about you and I would never betray you."

"Oh, I believe you, Fred. At least I believe that you mean it, if for no other reason than to implicate me is to implicate your own involvement. I do think you are the type of sentimental slob who would feel a sense of loyalty to a girl he'd been involved with. Life is complicated, Fred. Somewhere out there is a smart FBI agent who is on to me, sooner or later he or someone like him comes knocking on your door. Before you know it, they have everything you know about me, which is quite a lot, isn't it, Fred? We just can't have that. Don't worry, I'll be a lot easier on you in killing you than I was in bed with you last night."

"I won't leave then, I'll stay, I'll be your accomplice, I'll close my practice, sell my condo, come live with you, please, Ariella, please."

"Nah, it's too late for that, Fred. You would bolt at the first opportunity. I have no interest in keeping you locked up or on a leash. It's just easier to have you dead and out of the way. Sorry, Fred." She pointed the Beretta and fired.

The last thing I remember before darkness closed in was her saying, "Oh Fred, you've got blood all over my kitchen floor."

Forty-three
Hermosa Beach

It was over a month since Lindsay had seen Fred. She sensed something was wrong. She considered the possibility he might just have moved in with that Ariella girl, which somehow seemed unlikely. She saw their relationship as not likely to last and doubted a girl so glamorous could be so into Fred. Almost daily now she went by his condo on Third Street. His car was still parked in his spot and there was no sign of life anywhere inside.

She finally decided to check it out on her own. She was able to pick the cheap lock on the back door of the townhouse and let herself in. The place was a two-bedroom, two-story townhome with both bedrooms upstairs. She wandered through what seemed to be a very well-equipped kitchen for a bachelor, a living room area with a forty-eight-inch LED flat screen television and a small dining nook with a table accommodating two people. Upstairs one of the rooms was set up as an office. The phone on the desk was blinking from unanswered messages.

She turned on his computer and went through his e-mails. Most were work related but there were a few from someone named Eugene who appeared to be a friend, seemingly the only friend Fred had. There were no e-mails from Ariella or any other woman not associated with Fred's law practice. On his calendar there was a trip to Panama but that was over six weeks ago. He had no appointments or meetings scheduled over the last three weeks. There were bills and papers from work piled up on the desk but surprisingly little of a personal nature.

In the bedroom the bed was made and Fred's clothes were hung neatly in his closet. For a guy living alone, the place was almost disturbingly neat and clean. She looked through a rolodex on Fred's desk to see if she could find a telephone number for this Eugene person but there were very few numbers there. She checked the contacts section on his computer but it was empty. She guessed he kept all his contact numbers on his cell phone and there was no trace of a cell phone anywhere in the apartment.

After she let herself out, she decided to wait one more week before going to the police. Maybe he would show up. He never did and finally, on her day off from the restaurant, she went to the Hermosa Beach police station. At the front desk she told them she wanted to report a missing person. They told her to take a seat and someone would be with her shortly. It was over a half hour before she was beckoned back into the offices behind the front desk. She sat down in front of a short, stocky, Japanese-American girl dressed in slacks and a blouse. The nameplate on her desk read "Det. Anne Tamura."

"So, you're here about a missing person?" she asked.

"Yeah, a guy who lives on Third Street, he's been gone for over a month."

"Is he your boyfriend?"

"No, no, not at all, just a friend, a nice guy I play volleyball with. I think he's gotten himself involved with a pretty shady girl who might have done something to him."

Detective Tamura gave her a quizzical look.

"How do you know this guy is missing?"

"Well, he hasn't shown up to volleyball for over a month and, well, I've kinda been going by his place to see if he's around. No one is ever there but his car is always parked in his spot."

Detective Tamura raised her eyebrows slightly.

"What's this guy's name?"

"Fred Cornwall."

"Where does he work?"

"I don't know, he's a lawyer, he works downtown."

"You don't know whether or not he's been at work all this time?"

"No, I didn't know where to check."

"Well, we can track him down on the State Bar website. What's the name of this shady girl he's been involved with?"

"Ariella Blumkin, she went to the same high school I did. I've seen them together."

Detective Tamura once again lifted her head from her notes and looked appraisingly at Lindsay.

"What about other friends who might know where he is?"

"Well, he mentioned some guy named Eugene but I don't know his last name or where he lives."

"Okay, lastly give me Fred's address and the last time you saw him."

"He lives at 127 Second Street, unit C, and I last saw him sometime early last month, probably the first Sunday of the month. Oh, and detective, since he started dating this girl, he was showing up with bruises and stuff, even a black eye. I don't think that's a coincidence."

"Okay, Lindsay, I promise you we'll look into this as best we can. Come back in about ten days, ask for me and I'll give you a status report."

Lindsay left the station and went home to change to go to the beach. She was not sure she did the right thing by going to the police but she was glad the detective took her so seriously. She felt sure they would get to the bottom of the mystery of Fred's disappearance.

It was exactly ten days later when she went back to the Hermosa station and asked for Detective Tamura. This time the wait was even longer but after more than forty-five minutes she was ushered back to the same office.

"Hi, Miss Carpenter," said the detective. "We have had a chance to look into this Fred Cornwall a little bit. Let me tell you what we've found out. First, we contacted the office where he works downtown. He told them a while back he would be gone for two weeks. That was five weeks ago and no one seems to be able to contact him. His cell phone appears to be dead and no one knows where he is. So, your initial instincts were correct. Fred Cornwall is indeed a missing person. We have no record of him leaving the country, other than a trip to Panama a couple of months ago from which he returned. We checked his apartment and vehicle. There was no sign of foul play but no clue as to where he might be. He doesn't appear to have any family locally and we are still trying to track down this friend, Eugene. We're not sure who he is. Now as to your Miss Blumkin, the last trace of her is her graduation from UCLA seven years ago. We have no current driver's license, no social security number, no passport, no phone records, no utilities, no evidence of residency or home ownership, no social media of any kind. If I had to hazard a guess, I'd say the woman is deceased. Are you sure you saw her?"

"Positive. We went to the same high school, well for a year anyway, and she was kind of well-known because she was extremely pretty and kind of weird. I saw her pick Fred up in a gray Camry. There is no doubt in my mind it was her."

"Did you get a plate number on the gray Camry?"

"No, I didn't think it would be important and I just happened to pass by when she picked him up. Can you trace it?"

"Do you have any idea how many gray Camrys are registered in Southern California? You say she was weird. In what way?"

"Well, you know, she kept to herself, didn't date or participate in school activities, wasn't friendly. Her parents were Russian. They kept her on a really short leash, couldn't go to parties or go out had to be home early, stuff like that. I heard she beat up another girl who was teasing her, really did a number on her. Later someone told me her whole family, except her of course, was murdered."

"Yeah, we know about that. We also have no evidence this girl still exists, didn't move back to Russia or something. She seems like a dead end."

"I saw her."

"I know you think you did. That's the only evidence we have she still exists or is still around in Southern California. Look, we will continue to look into this. We're not letting it go. A missing person can be hard to track. You may have to prepare yourself for the possibility he's been murdered somewhere and his body hidden. That's the worst case. It maybe he just ran off with this beautiful girl you saw and neglected to tell anyone where he was going. I hope we can find out but I can't make any promises."

Forty-four
Mid-Wilshire District, Los Angeles

The jacaranda trees were in bloom on Eugene's street, beautiful purple blossoms adding some color to an otherwise drab street. Of course, when the blossoms fell on your car, they were full of a sticky pollen that could be a nuisance to get off and there were so many trees on his street that it was impossible not to park under one. Eugene was home by himself reviewing a number of proposals for liability insurance for the company which employed him as risk manager. Every two years they did a thorough review of all policies, comparing premiums and coverage. It was very boring work but he was used to it and good at it.

He had been thinking about Fred. Eugene had not heard from the guy in over a month since he got back from Panama. They had exchanged a couple of e-mails and then Fred went silent, not returning calls or e-mails. He knew the guy was involved in this crazy relationship with some phantom woman. Actually, Eugene only half believed she was real, but it wasn't like Fred to suddenly go silent like that. He and Eugene had been friends for years. Each was the other's only true friend. He knew that even if Fred were furious at him, he wouldn't have cut him off like this. Besides there was no reason to think Fred was mad at him at all. Eugene was sure something weird happened but had no idea what it could be.

He had got up to get a glass of iced tea from the kitchen when he heard a knock at the door. He looked out the peephole to see a young woman standing on his stoop. He opened the door to find one of the most beautiful women he had ever seen standing there. She was about five foot seven with long, thick, black hair falling past her shoulder blades, pale delicate skin and huge, luminous blue eyes in a lovely face highlighted by thick, sensual lips and delicate, refined cheekbones. She was wearing heels, close-fitting designer jeans, a sleeveless black silk top and a gray hoodie with the hood down. "Are you Eugene?" she asked with a hint of an ambiguous smile.

"I am, can I help you?"

"Hi, I'm Ariella. We have a mutual friend in Fred Cornwall."

Eugene was stunned. This beauty was the girl Fred had been talking about forever? She actually existed?

"So, you're Ariella. I'm sorry, I was never quite sure you existed. Please come in. I was just thinking about Fred. I haven't heard from him in ages."

She stepped into his living room and he shut the door behind her.

"That's why I'm here. Fred is still stuck back in Panama and he wanted me to look in on you and let you know everything is okay."

"Oh, well, you didn't have to come all the way here, you could have just given me a call to let me know he's okay. I'm glad to hear it though."

"I know, I lost your number and at my house in Panama we don't have cell service. So, I just thought it would be easier to come by. I hope I'm not interrupting anything?" she said, looking around the condo.

"No, not at all, just a quiet evening doing some boring work. Can I offer you an iced tea? I'm so glad to meet you. You've been an important part of Fred's life lately and I kept on bugging him about when I would get to meet you. I have to say nothing he said did justice to how lovely you are."

"Why thank you, that's nice of you to say. No thanks on the iced tea, I'll just stay a minute." Eugene remarked to himself that those huge blue eyes remained expressionless and she kept that same vague smile while they talked.

"So, what's going on with you two? Last time Fred and I talked it seemed as if you might be ready to take your relationship to another level."

"Well, that's exactly what happened. We've definitely gotten to another place in our relationship. You guys are very good friends?"

"Oh yeah, we've known each other for years and we usually get together at least once or twice a week. That's why it's so weird I haven't seen or heard from him in over a month. I don't think that has ever happened before."

"Would you say you're Fred's only friend or are there others?"

"Well, he plays volleyball every Sunday with a bunch of beach people but I don't really think you'd call them friends. I mean, yeah, I'm probably his only real friend and, if I'm honest, he's probably my only real friend, you know?"

"Well, Fred and I are alike in not being social types. We both like to keep to ourselves. I'll bet Fred hasn't even mentioned me to anyone else but you since we started dating."

"I wouldn't be surprised. I can't imagine who else he would tell, to be honest."

"Fred talked a lot about me with you, didn't he?"

"Oh yeah, every time we would get together the past few months you were all we would talk about. I heard all about your dates and stuff."

"I'm sorry about that, Eugene," she said with that ambiguous smile still on her face.

"No reason to be sorry, it was all good. The guy is crazy about you. He thinks you're wonderful."

"No, I mean I'm sorry I'm going to have to kill you, Eugene. You know a bit too much about me," she said, removing a pistol with a long black metal extension on the barrel from her purse and aiming it at him.

Eugene suddenly realized she was wearing gloves even though it was a warm evening. Before he could say a word, the gun made a muted popping sound and Eugene fell to the floor with a hole in his forehead. She zipped up her hoodie, put the hood over her head, checked the street outside through the front window and let herself out the front door.

Forty-five
New York City

Agent Ed Sanchez walked the corridor from the offices of the Argentine delegation to the viewing gallery for the U.N. General Assembly. The Italian suit he was wearing was much nicer than the off-the-rack Men's Wearhouse suits he usually wore. It contained a discreet body camera broadcasting to a remote monitor being viewed by Agent Chandler Diaz and several other agents.

While Sanchez was in the U.N. building with its tight security, he felt safe, but when he stepped outside, he knew he was a target.

Each day, so far, that he played the role of Pablo Corrales, Argentinian special envoy to the U.N., he had been genuinely terrified. The bulletproof vest he wore under his white dress shirts would not stop a shot to the head or a blade to the throat. The agents who shadowed him might not be quick enough to stop a killer before his work was done. This was easily the most difficult and dangerous assignment he had been given since joining the Bureau. Everything he had been told about this killer or killers was that they were professional, efficient. They had been paid one hundred thousand dollars to kill him with a promise of another hundred thousand when the job was finished. That thought gave him no comfort.

The Argentinian delegation, who agreed to help the FBI, were friendly and welcoming, though they made fun of his Puerto Rican Spanish. They gave him a desk and cubicle, accepted his comings and goings. He made a point of leaving the building for lunch each day to make himself available as a target. Each night he dined with other agents dressed as diplomats in nice restaurants. It would have been a nice perk of the job if fear had not dulled his appetite. Each morning he had a light breakfast in the hotel coffee shop and walked across the plaza to the U.N. headquarters.

So far there had been no sign of any killer. Diaz was clear to mention the killer might try to strike in a variety of ways. Sanchez should be wary of maids, janitors and waiters. He was advised not to eat the food or drink the beverages he ordered in restaurants. Another agent would anonymously order for him.

Diaz followed Sanchez's movements carefully, only briefly handing monitoring duties over to another agent to take short naps. So far there had been no sign of anyone stalking Sanchez. There were only two days left in the window the killer had been given so the entire team was on full alert. Diaz sent an e-mail to medusa199 asking what was going on and warning that the window for action was closing. The only response was *"acknowledged."*

The operation continued for the final two days. Every hour the tension among the team rose as the likelihood of an attack on Sanchez increased. The agents shadowing him kept a little closer and had their eye on anyone who looked even moderately suspicious. Nothing happened. Finally, at midnight of the final day they ferried Sanchez to JFK where he boarded a flight ostensibly bound for Buenos Aires. Sanchez actually left the aircraft before it took off, dressed as a crew member servicing the aircraft.

Diaz gathered the team in a conference room in the basement TSA headquarters and thanked them for their efforts. One hundred thousand dollars of Agency funds and many man-hours of valuable agent time had been expended on an operation that had been a total failure. Diaz did not look forward to the reaction of his supervisors.

With the operation officially terminated, the New York-based agents, including Ed Sanchez, returned to their homes. Diaz went back to Manhattan to his hotel. He would return to D.C. in the morning. Before he went up to his room, he stopped in the hotel lobby bar to have a drink to take the edge off his exhaustion and disappointment. He sat at the bar and ordered a Jack Daniels on the rocks. Down the bar from him he noticed a stunning blonde woman sipping a glass of club soda. She caught him glancing at her and smiled back. He smiled at her and she came down the bar and sat next to him. "Can I buy you a drink?" she asked.

Diaz reflected that on this, the worst day he had in the last five years, this exquisite woman would rescue the day by offering to buy him a drink. "I'd be delighted," he answered, carefully looking her over.

She was in her late twenties, blonde, pale skinned with huge blue eyes. She wore a black sleeveless dress, belted at the waist and hemmed well above her knees, showing off spectacular legs in patent leather stiletto heels. She ordered another club soda and a bourbon on the rocks for him. He briefly wondered if she were a high-class hooker but there was something about her which made him think not.

"I'm just in town for a couple of days on business. How about you?" she asked him.

"The same. In fact, we just finished up a project we were working on. I'll be going home tomorrow morning."

"Where's that?"

"D.C. I work for the Bureau."

"The FBI? How exciting. What kind of cases do you work on?"

"I'm in a special homicide division. We investigate high-profile murders. Like that hedge fund guy, Paul Voca, who was murdered a while back here in New York."

"Never heard of him, was he some sort of big shot?"

"Yeah, a guy with a reputation for taking over companies and gutting them. Not a very popular man but he controlled hundreds of millions of dollars. What do you do?"

Diaz reflected that he rarely talked agency shop with non-agents but the two bourbons were relaxing him and it was hard not to separate himself from the intense stakeout they had been running for days now.

"I'm a sort of consultant, kind of a Human Resources type. I help people with personnel problems, that sort of thing. Not anywhere as interesting as what you do. Where are you from originally?"

"Miami. I grew up there, my dad was Cuban, my mom American. She was shot in a robbery, died shortly after. That's when I decided to go into law enforcement."

"I'm so sorry for your loss but it sounds like you made something positive out of tragedy. That's impressive. So, did you ever catch the one who killed this Voca guy?"

"No, that's why I'm here in New York. We thought we were setting a trap for him but he never showed up."

"Maybe you didn't wait long enough?" she said putting her hand lightly on his arm.

He realized he shouldn't be telling her all this but the combination of fatigue, disappointment, the bourbon and this very attractive woman had loosened his tongue. "How about another bourbon?" she asked, noting that his glass was empty.

"I really should be getting back to my room. I have an early flight in the morning."

"Well, maybe we could take this conversation up to your room, if you're interested?"

She was smiling but there was a blankness in her large blue eyes that, had he been less drunk and tired, he might have found disturbing.

"Let's do that," he said, looking forward to getting a better look at the curvy body under that black dress. As they walked to the elevator he said, "My name's Chandler, by the way."

"Nice to meet you, Chandler. My name's Maria."

When they got to his room, he went to get a bottle of Irish whiskey he had and some clean glasses from the bathroom. When he came out with the glasses, she was aiming a pistol with a silencer at his chest.

"It's Maria Guisado, actually, Agent Diaz. You've done a nice job tracking me down and setting a trap for me but you made one mistake. I meticulously research every target I'm given. You and your team did a poor job of setting up background on Pablo Corrales. I'm fluent in Spanish and I found very little other than your shadow background on Corrales online and in the Argentine press. He seemed to have no history in Argentina other than a brief biography on the Argentine State Department web page. You picked a Puerto Rican agent to play Corrales who looks and sounds Puerto Rican. Argentines have a different ethnic background from Puerto Ricans. They speak a different strain of Spanish with a distinctly different accent and vocabulary. That's why your trap failed and why you were on your way to get reamed out by your bosses tomorrow. You're good, Agent Diaz, good enough to get close and to make you worth eliminating. Anyway, your Bureau paid me one hundred thousand dollars. It wouldn't be fair if they didn't get a killing in return, would it? When a client pays top dollar, they shouldn't be left empty handed. We aim to please."

Diaz went for the gun in his hip holster but she quickly fired and hit him in the middle of his forehead. He fell, instantly dead.

Forty-six
Buena Vista, Panama

My mother used to tell me an old Russian proverb "Сколько волка ни корми, он всё в лес смотрит." Roughly translated, it means "the wolf being fed enough nevertheless is looking to the woods." In other words, a wolf is always a wolf no matter what you do to change him. That was true of poor Fred and it's true of me, although of course I am really the wolf and Fred was more like a sheep. I was unable to make him more wolf-like.

A very weak breeze is floating up the hill as I lay by the pool reading *El Aleph* by Borges in Spanish. An ice bucket with a bottle of Mumm sits beside me. I can never really get enough champagne. I drink it constantly when I'm not working.

Lately I've been worried about the extradition laws here in Panama. I used to think that I could easily bribe any law enforcement types who came to arrest me and maybe that's still true. However, my lawyer here says that there is an old extradition treaty with the United States which authorizes extradition for capital crimes.

I've never killed anyone in France and they apparently don't readily extradite to the U.S., especially if it is for a capital crime and never if you are a French citizen. I think of that film director convicted of raping a child in California who is still living comfortably in Paris. There are French islands in the Caribbean that might do very nicely as a refuge. I'll have to look into that very soon.

The champagne bottle is empty and I no longer have Fred to scuttle into the kitchen and fetch another. Anyway, it's time to take a break from Borges and go see if the orchid is still there. I slip a cover-up over my naked body and put on my flip-flops. A toucan flies overhead as I stride down the hill toward the tree line. I love the silence and smell of the jungle. As I enter, the sun is covered and I walk through a dim forest of filtered light. Butterflies flit by, small yellow ones and a giant blue Morpho.

The first clearing I come to is where I buried Fred. I don't usually have to worry about disposing of bodies. I leave them where I kill them. Fred was a kind of personal kill. I had to drag him down the hill through the trees until I found a place with room to dig a shallow grave. The guy was heavier than he looked. There were a lot of things about Fred that were deceiving. Who would have thought submissive Fred might balk at assisting in a kill? I thought he worshipped me, would do whatever I asked, but the guy had principles. Did he really think I would just let him walk out? Of course, there is the heart of the problem. Fred had no clue who he was dealing with. He looked at me as a desirable woman. Of course, I am, but in the scheme of things I think of that as more of a fortunate accident having little to do with who I really am.

People don't expect women, especially beautiful women, to be dangerous. Even that agent Diaz thought he was looking for a man, which is why, when I picked him up in a bar, he took me to his hotel room without hesitation. Talk about opening doors. Yeah, beauty does that, but it also masks the person behind the beauty. For me that's been a good thing but I suspect for other women it might not be so desirable as you might think.

Already over the small mound that is Fred's last resting place there are plants and grasses covering the once-bare earth. I do miss Fred. There were times when it was nice to have a companion. Yes, we were uniquely sexually compatible and that is important. Sometimes it was just nice to have someone to watch a movie with, take a walk on Cabrillo beach, sit and listen to Charlie Parker with.

My late boyfriend, the UCLA Russian literature professor, called me a psychopath. Hey, maybe I am. Andrei, for all his faults, was, after all, a pretty perceptive guy. I admit I've always been different.

My mother said I lacked empathy. Clearly, she was right about that. I have problems feeling anything. I've never had a need for friends of either sex. I don't find that the feelings or the plight of others do much to move me. Don't psychopaths need love, too? I don't mean feeling love, just receiving it.

I move on after pausing at Fred's grave. By my next trip here it will be unrecognizable. There will eventually be someone else. Maybe next time I'll find someone even more pliable than Fred. Of course, I don't want an utter fool. Fred's problem was he could never see me for who I was until it was too late. He lost his nerve. I need someone with a bit more malleable morality.

The jungle thickens here. I can hear cicadas and the calls of birds through the silence. The vegetation closes in on me and the smell is musty and stale. I rarely sweat, but in the humidity of the forest, I do feel a few rivulets of sweat roll down my back and form under my arms. Next time I come this way, I may have to bring a machete.

Finally, I emerge in the clearing of the orchid. The dark blossom is nowhere to be seen but the stem of the plant is still there with a few thick dark leaves. I'm no botanist but I know the orchid will be back. Like me this black orchid is resilient, like me, it is beautiful and sinister.

About the Author

Robert V. Wadden, Jr. is a retired lawyer with a Master's in Literature from UCLA, currently splitting his time residing in the Los Angeles area and his house in Esterillos, Costa Rica.

Also by the Author
at
Rogue Phoenix Press

Curse of Ciudad Blanca

Peter VanOwen is living by the beach in Costa Rica when his old college roommate, a disgraced professor of archaeology, drops in unexpectedly to convince him to go on an expedition to discover a lost city in the Honduran jungle and help resurrect his career. He is enticed to join the expedition by the prospect of seeing once again his long-lost college girlfriend who has remained the love of his life. But once in Honduras he encounters a sinister and mysterious woman who entraps him into going on an expedition he had intended to avoid. Upon penetrating deep into the Honduran jungle in search of the lost city VanOwen comes face to face with a sinister reality that will change his life and that of his family, friends and even his ex-girlfriend.

One
PLAYA ESTERILLOS, COSTA RICA

The rainy season always made his joints ache. Almost every afternoon the clouds gathered over Playa Esterillos, slowly darkening until the sky exploded with thunder, lightning and rain often lasting all night. Peter loved the pounding rain on the tin roof of his roasting shed and the acrid smell of roasting coffee over the humid air.

When he was not visiting coffee growers in the central highlands, he followed the same routine each day. In the warm, dry mornings he stepped out of his compound onto the empty, grey sand beach. He would bring a thermal pot of coffee and lie on his chaise longue reading from his Kindle. Occasionally he entered the warm, calm water. By eleven AM he left the beach to fix a light lunch and check his computer for e-mails. In the afternoon as the humidity rose and the clouds gathered, he would retreat to his roasting shed to sample and experiment with the coffee beans he was considering recommending to his clients in the U.S.

The current batch of beans was from the area around San Vito, a town settled in the nineteen-fifties by Italian immigrants in the southern mountains of central Costa Rica. The beans were plump with promise: smooth and blue-green. His challenge was to find the ideal roast by roasting small batches to various levels, experimenting with temperature and duration. In his shed, he had a small one-kilo Diedrich sample roaster powered by propane. Peter spent his afternoons in the shed roasting batch after batch, sampling the results and recording his findings. He loved the smell, texture and sound of the beans as they progressed through the roasting process.

For Peter, coffee roasting was an escape. Immersion in the process let him lose himself in something outside himself. The deep calm he felt as he processed each batch was the result of escaping his own consciousness and savoring the details of the roast. When the results were good, when he had extracted the ideal balance between body and flavor for the particular bean, he felt a deep sense of satisfaction and accomplishment unconnected with the objective importance of well roasted coffee.

In an earlier life, Peter VanOwen had been a lawyer employed by the Los Angeles County Counsel's office. For a while he had a wife and children and a small house in a Los Angeles suburb. A rancorous divorce and early retirement led him to Costa Rica and a stucco house in a gated compound on the grey volcanic beach of Playa Esterillos on the Pacific coast. He had stumbled into coffee brokering more as a way to fill his days than a need to make money. But he had come to love the process and discovered in himself an entrepreneurial side which had lain dormant over his years as a public lawyer. He bought coffee from small growers and sold it to several modest-sized coffeeshop chains in the United States with recommendations on the roast and brewing. He often travelled throughout the central Costa Rican highlands looking for beans and occasionally travelled to Guatemala and Panama. Several times a month he would drive to San José to meet buyers. In between trips, he settled into his comfortable daily routine, seldom communicating with any of his old family and friends in California. His simple, isolated life suited him and he rarely felt a moment of loneliness. He loved the tropical weather, green, lush foliage and the easy, unhurried pace of Costa Rica.

Playa Esterillos had its share of American émigrés but Peter avoided them, as well as the nearby surfer town of Jaco with its high-rise hotels, surf shops and fish taco joints. He drank at home, not wanting to engage in the banal and self-promoting conversation of the typical American bar in Costa Rica. At 60 he had, he admitted to himself, become withdrawn and introspective.

As he watched the temperature on the Diedrich, Peter heard a car pull into his drive. He walked to the shed window to see a hired van expel a slight man with dark rimmed-glasses and ginger-colored hair, a man whom Peter had not seen for many years.